T0285580

Parade

Parade
Rachel Cusk

Farrar, Straus and Giroux
New York

Farrar, Straus and Giroux
120 Broadway, New York 10271

Printed in the United States of America
Originally published in 2024 by Faber & Faber Ltd, Great Britain
Published in the United States by Farrar, Straus and Giroux
First American edition, 2024

Library of Congress Cataloging-in-Publication Data
Names: Cusk, Rachel, 1967– author.
Title: Parade : a novel / Rachel Cusk.
Description: First American edition. | New York : Farrar, Straus
    and Giroux, 2024.
Identifiers: LCCN 2024006645 | ISBN 9780374610043 (hardcover)
Subjects: LCGFT: Novels.
Classification: LCC PR6053.U825 P37 2024 | DDC 823/.914—
    dc23/eng/20240214
LC record available at https://lccn.loc.gov/2024006645

Our books may be purchased in bulk for promotional,
educational, or business use. Please contact your local bookseller
or the Macmillan Corporate and Premium Sales Department at
1-800-221-7945, extension 5442, or by email at
MacmillanSpecialMarkets@macmillan.com.

www.fsgbooks.com
Follow us on social media at @fsgbooks

1   3   5   7   9   10   8   6   4   2

Parade

The Stuntman

At a certain point in his career the artist G, perhaps because he could find no other way to make sense of his time and place in history, began to paint upside down. At first sight the paintings looked as though they had been hung the wrong way round by mistake, but then the signature emblazoned in the bottom right-hand corner clearly heralded the advent of a new reality. His wife believed that with this development he had inadvertently expressed something disturbing about the female condition, and wondered if it might have repercussions in terms of his success, but the critical response to the upside-down paintings was more enthusiastic than ever, and G was showered with a fresh round of the awards and honours that people seemed disposed to offer him almost no matter what he did.

They lived in a region of forests some distance from the city, for despite its approval of him G was angry and hurt by the world and could not bring himself to forgive it. His early work had been brutally criticised, and though people assured him that his power to shock was the surest proof of his talent, G had not recovered from these attacks. His was the type of strength not to withstand attempts to poison and destroy him but rather to absorb them, to swallow the poison and be altered by it, so that his survival was not a story of mere resilience, but was instead a slow kind of crucifixion that eventually compelled the world to chastise itself for what it had done to him. It was because of the forests that G had found a way out of his artistic impasse, caught as he had felt himself to be between the anecdotal nature of representation and the disengagement of abstraction. He had spent a great deal of time observing the activities of the local foresters, and each time he saw a tree being felled this question of verticality had suggested itself to him. First he had painted the men and the trees in a sort of joint condition of existence, in which the trunks were interchangeable with the bodies. Then he had seen how the bodies too could be felled, severed from their own root and likewise turned on their side or cut into sections. The notion of inversion finally came to him as a means of resolving this violence and restoring the principle of wholeness, so that the world was once more intact but upside down and thus free of the constraint of reality.

When G's wife first saw the upside-down paintings she felt as though she had been hit. The feeling of everything seeming right yet being fundamentally wrong was one she powerfully recognised: it was her condition, the condition of her sex. The paintings made her unhappy, or rather they led her to acknowledge the existence of an unhappiness that seemed always to have been inside her. G made a painting she particularly loved, of slender birch trees in sunlight, and the demented calmness and innocence of these upside-down trees seemed to suggest the possibility of madness as a kind of shelter. How had he understood this nameless female unhappiness inside her that made madness such a temptation? Unlike other artists they knew, G could not have been accused of exploitation: he didn't suffer from blind male self-importance, and nor had he ever taken any kind of liberty that the public value of his gaze might have seemed to legitimise. He had told her that before he met her he had resorted greatly to masturbation. Was he in fact claiming this marginal perspective as his own? If so he had had to lay down his masculinity, however temporarily, to claim it. He had approached the marginal sidlingly, as it were from a sideways direction, participating in its disenfranchisements, in its mute and broken identity, with the difference that he had succeeded in giving it a voice.

The early paintings were large portraits, fluid and somewhat naive in style, of recognisable individuals from their region and from the circle of their acquaintance. They were simple and formal, as though G were making a statement about his own honesty at the very moment that he was turning the world upside down. Why were these people upside down? It was all one could ask, yet the answer seemed so obvious, it felt as though any child could answer it, and so the paintings succeeded in illuminating a knowledge that the person looking at them already possessed. G began to paint large, intricate landscapes in which nature seemed to be in its heyday, seemed to speak of its power of recovery from human violence, its vigil through successive dawns to re-emerge perennially into the light. It basked in a wordless moral plenitude, innocent and unconscious of the complete inversion it had undergone, and it was this quality of innocence, or ignorance, that succeeded in entirely detaching the representational value of the painting from what it appeared to represent.

The question of whether G was actually painting an inverted world, or had simply turned the paintings on their heads and signed them when they were finished, was subject to a curious silence. The first scenario represented a formidable technical challenge; the second was more of an absurdist joke that could be passed off in a matter of minutes. Yet he was never publicly interrogated about it, and the question went unmentioned in the many critical writings about this radical development in his work. Sometimes people asked G's wife about it in private, as though in her presence they were finally safe to risk a display of stupidity. In such moments she felt realised in her role as a repository for weakness. She didn't resent it, because one learned so much more this way, but it summed something up for her, and not just about art, that so enormous a confusion around the truth could remain veiled in tacit muteness. She guessed this was how everything that was noble was eventually destroyed. G would have agreed with her wholeheartedly, and in fact she noticed that he began to speak openly about his technique of his own accord, explaining the difficulties of inverted painting that could be resolved only through the use of photographs. Later he rejected the photographic medium and the paintings became even larger and more dreamlike and abstract. The question of what a human being actually was had never seemed so unanswerable in any case. He often painted a man cowering alone in bed, the sullied oceanic blankness of the sheets, with the little tormented man somewhere at the top of the frame.

G believed that women could not be artists. As far as G's wife was concerned this was what most people believed, but it was unfortunate that he should be the one to say it out loud. She wondered whether it was her own indefatigable loyalty to him, her continual presence by his side, that had brought him to this view. Without her, he might still be an artist but he would not really be a man. He would lack a home and children, would lack the conditions for the obliviousness of creating, or rather would quickly be destroyed by that obliviousness. So she thought that what he was really saying was that women could not be artists if men were going to be artists. Once, she was in his studio for the visit of a female novelist, who was struck as though by lightning by the upside-down paintings, much as G's wife had been herself. I want to write upside down, the woman exclaimed, with considerable emotion. No doubt G found this a preposterous thing to say, but G's wife was quietly satisfied, because she herself felt that this reality G had so brilliantly elucidated, identical to its companion reality in every particular but for the complete inversion of its moral force, was the closest thing she knew to the mystery and tragedy of her own sex. There had been a plaintive note – of injustice, perhaps – in the novelist's tone, as though she had just realised something had been appropriated from her. G was not the first man to have described women better than women seemed able to describe themselves.

The lady had asked us to leave, for suddenly she wanted her apartment back. There could be no delay in satisfying this desire – though we had nowhere else to go, we must be gone straight away. We had lived there for more than a year: the walls of the apartment had been our safety in the move to this foreign city. We felt sheltered there, high up on the top floor where we could open the windows and look down at the street without being seen ourselves. After we left, the lady would sometimes call us out of the blue, to find out how we were getting on. She made sure to sound casual and friendly, but the calls themselves spoke of guilt.

There had been a mirror in that apartment, ornate and gilded, that was so large it reflected the looker not as the centre of the image but as part of a greater scene. To look in it was to be seen in proportion to other things. The loss of the mirror was like the loss of a compass or navigation point. It was surprising how deeply it had bestowed a feeling of orientation. Sometimes a minor change can bring down a major structure, and this was the case with the lady's apartment. After we left, a number of things happened whose roots, when you unearthed them, could usually be found there. It was reported to us that the lady had not remained long in her apartment after all. It had disappointed her in some way, so she had gone back to where she had been living before and now it stood empty. She had cultivated an image, perhaps, of her old life in the apartment that had drawn her away from the new life she had established elsewhere. But the apartment, when she got there, did not contain the old life. The old life had become the new life that she was already living.

For several weeks we stayed in one place after another, never unpacking our suitcases. We were natives neither of the city, nor of the country itself, nor of its language: the lady's apartment had been like a boat, and now we were cast into the sea. It had been full of her possessions, and I had derived a deep security from living among her things, which were of a kind I would not have chosen myself. It was not only the liberation from my own tastes and preferences that had comforted me, but also the immersion in the sensibility of another. I did not, in fact, need to ask myself why it felt so pleasant to live in a world created by someone else. Yet that same surrender, in the places that followed, was increasingly disturbing. We spent a lengthy period in a small blank apartment where the occupant of the rooms overhead paced the floors rapidly and ceaselessly every hour of every night, and I was drawn into the inquietude of this unseen stranger, which came to seem like my own inquietude – suppressed for the past year – awakening. The only mirror was a rectangle above the bathroom sink, and the front door was fitted with a succession of heavy steel locks, as though the concept of individuality had all at once become more limited and more threatened.

Nearby there was a park where a great cherry tree

grew. Its giant boughs were so ancient and so heavy that they rested all around it on the ground. In the sudden sunshine of the premature spring the tree had blossomed and given forth a startling white foam of flowers like the breaking of an enormous wave. The blossoms made a bridal canopy around the trunk that undulated and rippled in the breezes. This canopy was so large that it formed a sort of shelter, like a tent around the huge gnarled trunk. I thought often of the home we had left, our own home, left of our own volition.

We moved to another temporary apartment and then another. We stayed for a few nights in a place with a broken boiler, where we could not remove our coats. Rain and freezing sleet hurled themselves from the sky, a reprise of winter. I thought of the cherry tree in the park that had put out its blossom so early. In the streets people were sleeping huddled in doorways or under bridges and walkways, or sometimes in tents they had pitched on the pavements. Everyone walked past them, these reproaches to subjectivity, with apparent indifference. We ourselves, outsiders, in a limbo of our own making, perhaps felt the reproach differently. At home people also slept in doorways: here it took us longer to forget them.

We moved from place to place until spring returned for good and the trees regained their foliage and the streets became lively again. Walking through the city in the fierce fresh sunlight, the element of freedom in our rootlessness could intermittently be felt. We had finally found somewhere to live, an apartment of our own, which would be available in a few weeks. With this harbour in sight, our true feelings – which bore now the toll of experience – became more evident. A certain bloom – an innocence, or perhaps just an ignorance – had been stripped from us. We had envisioned a life here in this city and then we had gone about trying to make the vision real, and in that process the role of imagination appeared especially ambiguous, appeared to have exposed something we hadn't known about our relationship to reality itself. This other death-face of imagination flashed before us now and then, in the periods when one thing could not be linked to another and a lack of sequence or logic was apparent in the enactment of our plans.

One morning, walking along a quiet sunny street where people sat at pavement tables drinking coffee, I was attacked by a stranger who hit me forcibly in the head. My assailant was a woman, deranged by madness or addiction, and this fact of her gender caused difficulties both in the recounting of the event afterward and in my own response to it. I had not noticed her approach or prepared myself for the blow, which left me bleeding on my hands and knees in the road with no understanding of what had happened. A crowd instantly gathered: people rose from their tables, shouting and gesticulating. In the pandemonium the woman walked away. The onlookers were pointing at her: she had stopped on the street corner and turned around, like an artist stepping back to admire her creation. Then she shook her fist in the air and she vanished.

It occurred to me in the time that followed that I had been murdered and yet had nonetheless remained alive, and I found that I could associate this death-in-life with other events and experiences, most of which were consequences in one way or another of my biological femininity. Those female experiences, I now saw, had usually been attributed to an alternate or double self whose role it was to absorb and confine them so that they played no part in the ongoing story of life. Like a kind of stuntman, this alternate self took the actual risks in the manufacture of a fictional being whose exposure to danger was supposedly fundamental to its identity. Despite having no name or identity of her own, the stuntman was what created both the possibilities and the artificiality of character. But the violence and the unexpectedness of the incident in the street had caught my stuntman unawares.

Even after we had moved into our apartment I was unable to forget or recover from what had happened, and the pure sorrow I felt seemed to stem from the consciousness of a larger defeat to which this incident had contributed the decisive stroke. The blow itself, which both belonged to memory and stood outside it, could not be digested: it stuck as though in the throat, impossible either to swallow or to spit out. Those few seconds repeated themselves over and over before my mind's eye, like something trapped and unable to find an exit, and the question of who my assassin was, of why she had attacked me and what it was she had seen in me that she wanted to break, gradually gave way to the knowledge that what I was experiencing was the defeat of representation by violence.

When the lady next called, I took a perverse kind of pleasure in telling her my news. How awful! she shrieked. I noticed she ended the call more quickly than usual. I guessed we wouldn't hear from her again.

G decided to paint his wife in something approximating the classical manner, as a nude. But the paintings were chaotic and dark: far from freeing him from subjectivity, inversion seemed merely to disclose an unpleasantness inside himself, a crystallised hatred that both objectified his wife and obliterated her. She couldn't be seen, or at least not by him: something brutal in their contract, the contract of marriage, surged forth and shattered the perceptual plane. It was not unusual for violence to spill out of the upside-down paintings, but it was a violence that he already knew he contained: he had inherited it, could answer it, was occasionally its victim; what he did not desire was to become it.

G and his wife went to visit G's father, who lived in a stuffy little room in a retirement home out in flat countryside. It was difficult to find reasons to visit him, since the home was not near or on the way to anywhere that G and his wife ever wanted to go. Yet at one time his domination of G had been such that it was indistinguishable from fate. There had been a period of years in which G and the father had not spoken, an estrangement for which G's father blamed him entirely, while also appearing to be perfectly content with it. His lack of self-reproach was more tormenting to G than almost anything else. There were stories of people who were redeemed by the approach of death and the light it shed on the truth. G had believed the father could never die because it was impossible he would be redeemed in this way. Then one day he had summoned G to the stuffy room out in the flat countryside, and so it seemed that after all he would die. G was privately frightened of going. He believed the father might kill him, annihilate him as he had once created him. Then G's wife had said that she would come. It was surprising to discover this insurance policy of marital love, which he had never thought to count on. Now she always accompanied him on these visits.

The father was standing red-faced at his window, which looked out on the small round lawn and the drive-way and the winding access road that came across the flat fields in front of the building. In the centre of the round lawn was a bare weeping willow. When the father saw them arrive he moved away from the window, where the winter sun made hard geometric shapes on the glass. His furious red face had seemed trapped behind the shapes but now it was gone. The empty glass glittered. Later, during their visit, he returned several times to that window to look out. It seemed to be a territorial instinct that was also a compulsion of memory, as though he were being forced to carry the burden of memory to the window to offer it up.

The room was on the second floor. Its thick beige car-pet gave off a chemical smell. There was also the slightly rancid smell of old age. Through the window the day was windless and still, and at the centre of the motionless scene the bare willow, now seen from above, stood in the pool of its own fallen leaves. The hard winter light filled the hot room. The father sat in a padded leather chair facing the window. There was a television set in the corner but the chair had been moved away from it.

The father did not watch television. Next to the chair was a varnished wooden side-table with a folded newspaper lying on it. The father's shrunken body was clad in a grey shirt tucked into belted corduroy trousers. The clothes hung from him, but there was still a toughness to his flesh. He wore an expression of astonishment that never altered. He had a history of participation in certain evils of which G knew only part, and against G he had committed many indelible acts of speech that remained uncorroded in G's recollection. They never changed or faded – it was the father who changed, as time ate away at him. G's growing inclination to forgive the father for the things he had said was also an inclination to forgive him for the things he had done, even though the first lay in the terrain of personal memory and the second in that of public record. But G had not succeeded in disentangling them, and together they filled him with such a darkness that his instinct was to rip them out of himself and fling them away without further examination.

G's wife moved around quietly at the other end of the room, preparing coffee in the small kitchenette. It was darker there and her form glimmered strangely among the slashing diagonals of light that reached it from the window. The winter sun was low and the petrifying white lines laid themselves over the cupboards and walls so that she was rayed like a zebra where she stood. The same distance that had beset G in the nude paintings was suddenly present here, in this oppressive room. His wife's freedom, so partial and malformed, had a crippling effect on him. She was only a few feet away. He could neither use her nor dispense with her, could not, because of her, be entirely free himself. It was her undeveloped equality with him that was crippling. She was not the pure object of his desire, nor was she his rival and equal in power. Instead she was his companion: she situated herself there, only a few feet away, in the terrain of weaknesses, of need, of plain daily requirements. Yet she herself could be desired – the father, for instance, was beadily watching her body move through the caressing bands of dark and light. Why did she not make proper use of her power, one way or the other? When G tried to see her, he simply saw his effect on her, saw in other words himself. Another man looking at her would see something different – this, he realised, was what he was unable to tolerate. It was unbearable that she could take his power of sight away from him and still be seen by everyone else. When he looked at her what he saw was his sexual failure as an animal, a failure brought about by the interference of society, of civilisation itself, in the courage and capacity of their own bodies. Perhaps men had always painted nudes in the same way as they committed violence – to prove that their courage had not been damaged by morality and need.

The father was talking in the monotone he had adopted in old age, the affectless flat tone of loneliness. G's wife would ask him the simplest question and the answer could last for fifteen minutes, the voice neither rising nor falling but moving steadily over the surface of things and levelling them, like a tank steadily reducing a field of action to flatness and dust. The regional accent of his youth that had lain dormant through all the years of his adult vigour had crept back into his voice. G heard in that accent the problem of history itself, as it insidiously bequeathed its dark inheritance to each unsuspecting new generation. G's wife had returned with the coffee and placed it on the low table in front of them. She sat down beside G on the small hard sofa. With her malformed freedom was she free also of history and of responsibility for the past? What had she herself inherited that bound her to the ongoing story of time? The father was looking at them, sitting there side by side. Together on the sofa, G and his wife now composed an image that told its own story, that could easily be read, unlike the image of minutes earlier, that of G's wife striped like a wild beast among the kitchen cupboards. Side by side on the sofa the question of her insufficient self-realisation – her lack of effort, as it were – was now out in plain sight, as was his own crippled courage. These were the fundaments of his discovery of inversion, because reality would always be better than the attempt to represent it, and the power of truth, which lay entirely in the act of perception, could stand free of that attempt. A feeling of immense relief passed through him. Tomorrow, when they were home again, he would start a new painting.

After I was hit, I desired for several weeks to hit in my turn. It was as if the violence were an actual object that had been transferred to me and that I needed to pass on. What I passed on would be more or less exactly what I had received – a blow to an unsuspecting stranger in the street. It would not, it seemed, have been altered in any way by its passage through my self. The only difference was that I had no feeling for – no interest in – the consequences of this action. I remembered the way my assassin had turned around, once she was at a safe distance, to look at what she had done.

We went away for a weekend to another city, to see an exhibition of works by the female sculptor G. The exhibition occupied the entire top floor of a grand museum, accessed by a broad walkway that circled a vast central atrium. Light cascaded from the glass ceiling down to the marble floor far below. Beyond the open doors of the entrance, where the attendant sat checking tickets, one of G's characteristic giant cloth forms could be seen hanging in space, suspended from the ceiling – a human form without identity, without face or features. It was genderless, this floating being, returned to a primary innocence that was also tragic, as though in this dream-state of suspension we might find ourselves washed clean of the violence of gender, absolved of its misdemean-ours and injustices, its diabolical driving of the story of life. It seemed to lie within the power of G's femininity, to unsex the human form.

A sickness had taken possession of me since the attack, of body but also of mind. The boundary of possi-bility had been moved, and the world was now a different place. Its properties had been inverted: the self and its preoccupations were shrunken and impotent, and the exterior plane with its prospects of imminent danger and disorder greatly enlarged. I watched people move blithely through their days, unconscious of what could at any moment befall them. It was from the impulse to wake them from this trance, perhaps, that my desire to hit was being generated. For the first time in years, I thought about the violence of childbirth, when I had passed as if through a mirror into an inchoate, animal region, a place with no words. A part of myself, I saw, had been abandoned there, the part played by the stuntman. But now my stuntman had stepped out of the shadows.

If the body was an object, could be treated as an object, the stuntman attained a new authority. It was she, not I, who now walked around in the guise of myself.

Yes, of course, I had thought when I awoke after a smashed interval to find myself lying in the street in blinding pain with no knowledge of how I had got there. Automatically I had tried to understand what had happened, where I was, as when one wakes in darkness in a strange room – as though the world, when unobserved, turns itself upside down and it is the task of human consciousness to right it. This awful effort, this responsibility to locate oneself in space and time and apply logic to one's situation, was somehow immensely pitiable. A crowd of people had gathered and in the moments before they began to react, they seemed simply to be looking at me as they might look at a picture in a museum. They were waiting for my reaction: they needed it, this representation, to be able to act themselves. Their instinct was to disown the violence or to pretend they hadn't seen it. It was up to me to place it in reality. I thought that I had perhaps been hit by a car, or that some heavy object had fallen on me from the buildings above, but the street was a pedestrian street and the paving stones were empty and clean. Then I remembered the woman I had glimpsed, shortly before turning to cross over to the other side. She had been standing ahead of me along the pavement beside some temporary railings that blocked the way forward. I had briefly registered her image and then instinctively turned away, out of politeness in order not to encroach on her, and remembering this I thought *yes, of course.*

Did I believe that being hit by a woman was my fault in a way being hit by a man could not have been? I could not have assigned meaning to being hit by a man, could have found no reason for him to hit me, and assigning meaning was my duty, just as it was my duty to get off my hands and knees and stand up. Why did it make sense for a woman to hit me? It was as though a violence underlying female identity had risen up and struck. This was the domain of the stuntman, this attack on me that had originated within myself, but now the stuntman seemed to have taken an actual human form and been externalised. In the exhibition I found different reflections of this notion, there in the vague and exalted light of those lofty silent rooms, which opened one upon another, so that one felt drawn deeper and deeper into G's secret being, where the making of art bore a relationship at once childlike and savage to the living of life. Here, sanity and insanity were not opposites but rather were the two faces of animate matter, the point at which the existence of consciousness can get no further in breaking down the existence of substance, of the body. Art, rooted in insanity, transforms itself through process into sanity: it is matter, the body, that is insane.

Inside a glass case, two headless knitted dolls were copulating: blindly driven by instinct and need, the body has no awareness of its own preposterousness. Beside them lay a row of little cloth women with pink doll-babies dangling from their groins by a knitted cord. Here and there stood G's hallmarks, the giant forms of black spiders, balanced on stiletto-like feet. Their insanity seemed to resemble the special insanity of the female body itself. Hideous and humble, incessantly fabricating, the spider's body doomed it to utility. The sculptures were a counter-fabrication: through the metamorphosis of art, the ugly insects became emblematic. They represented everything that is denied and suppressed in femininity, everything that remains darkly continuous behind its volcanic cycles of change and yet is unknown.

The exhibition was a memorial in thread and cloth, a knitted cathedral. How could the female sex be commemorated in stone? Its basis lies in repetition without permanence. Its elements are unlasting yet eternal in their recurrence, as violence itself is. This notion seemed to illuminate the germ of creativity in my assassin's blow. While I was sitting with the police, who had led me to a chair at one of the pavement tables, the proprietor of the cafe had come out to give me a glass of water. She was sympathetic and kind, bemoaning the number of crazy people on the streets, mentally ill people, addicts. She told me that my assassin had been hanging around this corner for three days, and that the previous afternoon she had hit a woman in exactly the same place and in exactly the same way that she had hit me. That square of pavement, with its temporary railings, was, then, my assassin's studio – she was making something there, something it would take several attempts to get right. Her actions made no sense, were apparently insane, and yet to me they were entirely comprehensible.

Coming out of the exhibition, we were met by a group of shock-faced attendants barring the way to the stairs. People were running and there was the sound of raised voices. The museum was being evacuated: the central staircase was closed off and the crowd was being directed to the fire exits. Outside we stood on the museum steps in the dusty sunshine. An ambulance was parked there and medics were rushing to and fro. We were told that a man had just thrown himself over the staircase outside the doors to the exhibition and fallen to his death on the marble floor of the atrium. A group of medics came out carrying the body on a stretcher and bore it past us. It was covered with a blue tarpaulin. Carried like that, the man seemed to have attained a shocking freedom. He had become a shape, already abstracted by the stiff blue shroud that wrapped him.

*

G's wife has a stomach-ache, a backache, a shooting pain in her hip when she gets too quickly out of a chair. Sometimes her hands shake in the mornings holding the coffee cup. She receives these complaints of the body mildly, without consternation. In her turn she commands herself to walk vigorously each day in the fields and woods near the house; she attends exercise classes and eats with care; she grants herself things that are warming and comforting, a hot bath, a rest in the afternoon. Often she and G travel to southern places, and she absorbs the brilliant sunlight and the smells and sensations of the sea until she becomes radiant. Through this combination of will and self-reward, her body passes its days. Their accumulation is a sort of secret history, a diary: unobserved, she pays a more or less continuous attention to herself that only hints at a greater lack of significance. Her children are adults now, and she looks back on her history with them in a fatigued kind of amazement, like a retired general recalling past battles. She continues to be a woman, yet that fact has lately met with some kind of constraint or opposition: instead of flowering and putting out its display, her femaleness is growing back into itself. Her body no longer represents any kind of danger.

For a long time she felt she had evaded G's knowledge of her. Some incapacity in him, which was perhaps a form of kindness or consideration, prevented him from knowing her completely. She evaded his possession while wanting him, in fact, to possess her. It had seemed to be her fault that she could not be possessed by him: it suggested that she lacked something in womanliness. But the terms of possession, for him, were not what she had thought. It was not easy to live with someone who saw so much in what he looked at. It seemed as though his gaze ought effortlessly to be able to devour her. So the fact that he did not, would or could not devour her constituted a rejection, as of something pushed to the side of the plate. Indignant, she silently held herself away from him. The nude paintings were in a way the account of this battle. Her separateness, so fracturing in his eyes, blackened the space between them: she was tarnished by it, blackened herself, looked at with suspicion. Yet there in the paintings was the boundary he himself would not cross. Sometimes, lying drowsily beside him in bed, she yearned for the description of herself that he refused to offer. He would not describe her while there was still a danger to himself, a risk.

The proposal of a double portrait did not especially alarm her: on the contrary, it suggested a solution to the impasse. His idea was that they should appear side by side, seated on a sofa or some such. She was interested to see what account he would give of himself, sitting

there beside her. She had assumed that this development had come from a compulsion toward honesty and
on that basis she took her place beside him on the sofa.
But it became clear that he didn't realise what he had
done to her with the nude paintings. He didn't know
that he had stolen something from her. He had made
her ugly, and he didn't know how angry and anguished it
had made her to be seen as ugly, when he was the single
being who might have been said to have an obligation to
find her beauty. The double portrait showed their living
room drenched in brilliant morning sun. The wallpaper
bore a blue-and-white pattern of flowers – she was not
sure she had ever been truly conscious of those flowers
until she saw them upside down and noticed their disturbing and livid aliveness. The furnishings were a little
faded, casually messy. The sofa cushions were creased.
The sun seemed to be leaching energy from the room in
the same moment as it illuminated it. The tall windows
in the background were opaque with light. At the centre
of the upside-down scene was a two-headed monster:
G and his wife, as creased and bleached as the cushions
they sat on. They were holding hands, loosely. Their hair
and clothes were untidy. Somehow, she had been captured.

He went further, suggesting they sit for the next portrait naked. She could have refused, but the moral logic

of her situation didn't allow it. He had amassed significant wealth by now, as well as fame, and her status as his companion and wife was of a more serious order. It was her duty to help him – nothing, not even love of their children, was as powerful as the obligation she felt toward his talent. His success – his achievement – was also hers, or rather she had relinquished any possibility of achieving something by giving her life and strength to him, and so she had claimed a part of it, his power, for herself. In that way she seemed no different from any other housewife: what she understood now was that the actual difference between her and those others belonged to him also.

He paints a whole sequence of the nude double portraits and when she looks at them she sees the spectacle of her own unrealised life. Just as she has been his point of access to the superficial world, so he is using her now to make his confession. Her body is a sort of shield that he holds in front of himself against the attack by time. Yet the implication is that their coexistence has been a fetter on his soul. There is something apparently humble, something almost comic in his willingness to present himself as one half of their couple. But the joke is on her. Bound to him, sitting in her place beside him, she has been turned upside down.

The portraits become bigger and more abstract: the two figures side by side are broken down into shapes, into disintegrating shadows that seem to be fading or reintegrating into the picture plane. She understands that he will continue to paint them, perhaps until the end. They are his late work, the melancholy song of his ageing, and the public consumes them more enthusiastically than ever, because this honesty in the face of time and death is what it cherishes the most. The fact that she herself is imprisoned in the paintings is the unerring mark of his originality. He appears to surrender something by including her, the pride of his masculinity and the egotistical basis of male identity. In this way he marks the end of history and the advent of a new reality. The ageing bourgeois couple trapped unto death in their godless and voluntary bondage is the pedestrian offspring of history.

Some days, in the city, all the children seem to be crying. They are wheeled along the streets in their chairs, wailing like sirens. Their tear-streaked faces can be seen through the windows of passing cars as they sob disconsolately in their car seats. In the park, in the supermarket, on the buses and trains, their sounds of lamentation fill the air, like those of seers who have glimpsed some unspeakable horror about to befall us. Their parents handle them with studied patience while not seeming to address the causes of their unhappiness. They bear them weeping through the streets, as though they are merely the caretakers of these beings whose sorrowful message is meant for us all.

Sometimes the screams reached the window of my room in the new apartment, where I was reading about G, a late-nineteenth-century woman painter dead of childbirth at the age of thirty-one. Her nude self-portraits show her heavily pregnant, her head inclined to meet her own eyes in the image. Can the element of the eternal in the experience of femininity ever be represented as more than an internalised state? G was trying to show herself from the outside, while she experienced the dawning knowledge of her situation and its consequences. She didn't entirely know quite what it was she had chosen: she was being led by instinct. To be led by instinct is the pre-eminent freedom attributed to male artists, and to the making of art itself. There is a self-destructive element to that instinct, and to the creative act, but in this case the cards have been dealt out in advance: G was stepping out of a relative safety and into the world of her own illegitimacy.

G often painted in dramatic close-up, for instance the mouth of a baby suckling a breast or a child's hands grasping a toy. She was making a point not just about lack of physical workspace and the inundation of that space by others, but about what a woman sees; not an artist, but a woman in the reality of her womanhood. For now, what she sees isn't terribly important, as she herself isn't terribly important – it's the implication of this step, this move into representation, that is radical. G lived in a milieu where the offer of equality was really an offer of imitation: painting schools for women, men who were prepared to teach in them, waves of artistic movements they could ride if they wished, and who could really have seen that there was something wrong in that, some fundamental falsification that would betray and poison the root of being that is the sole source of artistic worth?

G made a painting of her husband sleeping, and the whole history of women painted asleep in beds the artist has clearly just vacated was quietly mocked. The husband had fallen asleep fully clothed in a chair, in fact – he hadn't even taken off his glasses. The painting is an exercise in mild wonder, wonder at the familiarity and yet unknowability of this being, her husband, wonder perhaps at his entitlement to simply fall asleep like that, wonder at the artist's own power to perceive him when he doesn't know he's being watched, as women perceive their husbands from deep within their subjugation to them. It is not usual for a record to be made of those perceptions: G's point might have been that if one were to answer truthfully the question of what a female art might look like, it would have to be composed chiefly of a sort of non-existence. In the absence of an inviolable self, the making of art becomes something bound to the self in a more violent way, a kind of self-immolation or suicide mission: the body is one's only possession, and it must be given in exchange. She fulfilled both parts of this bargain, without necessarily expecting to.

Amid the children's screams, my own history of motherhood feels like something far upriver, from which I've drifted a long way – perhaps that is why the truth can no longer be detected there. Might it be possible to go beyond it in some broader sense, to surmount it, not just in time but also in actual meaning – in other words, to progress? The screaming children fill me with impatience and a sort of dread, as though they represent some universal task from which I will never be free. At night I frequently dream that someone has given me their baby to look after and disappeared. In these dreams I am not impatient: there is simply a harrowing anxiety. In the children's screams I hear something true, so true I want to block my ears, yet the world of domesticity and nurture they invoke, though irreducibly real, is a world submerged in and muffled by its enslavement to time, where that truth is held perennially at a distance. To be a mother is to live piercingly and inescapably in the moment. The artist who is also a mother must leave the moment in order to access a moment of a very different nature, and each time she does it a cost is exacted, the cost of experience. It is experience of almost too form-ative a kind, like being a soldier, and I am a veteran of it. I want medals, a special uniform. When the woman hit me in the street I felt a veteran's outrage at being attacked. It was only this, this part of myself that had been a mother, that was capable of outrage. The rest of me felt that it was what I deserved.

G painted herself dressed up as though to go out, a strange narrow painting, as if she were being looked at through a keyhole. Absurdly, she holds a lemon in her hand. The painting encapsulates the mystery and mel-ancholy of the transition toward self-being, its mixture of wonder and loneliness, its proximity to a kind of madness. In the coffin-like narrowness of the frame she poses, but for whom? The mild evasiveness of her expression is perhaps also a letting down of her guard – this is the expression she wears when no one is look-ing. With her yellow necklace and green cloak she seems almost to be in costume, half-ironically dressed up for the painting. But who is looking, noticing? The picture is asking a question about validity, the validity of this image, the validity of making it. The painter is also the subject, and in this moment they seem almost to can-cel each other out, to create a deeper kind of invisibility. Her death is not far away. Yet there is colour, brightness, volume – these things belong to the world. The yellows of the lemon in her hand and of her necklace together constitute stability: through this concrete existence and the existence of things, the painting can redeem itself, telling her to hang on.

G and his wife travel to Italy, to a cultural festival where G will be the guest of honour. It sounds like a glamorous invitation, but the festival is badly organised and the weather is unseasonably rainy and grey. There is a public interview with G, and fewer people attend than might have been expected. The villa where they are staying is a centre for artists' residencies – many, many years ago, when their children were very small, G came with his family here for several months. His time in this villa all those years ago was what helped to bring about the first great turning point in his work, as though in a foreign place he had finally been able to unchain himself from the predestination of identity and be free. It is for this reason – nostalgia, perhaps – that he accepted the invitation to the festival. But the villa is gloomy and uncomfortable and chilly: G and his wife, it seems, have grown accustomed to greater luxury. G rails and is angry; he catches a cold and cancels his media appointments. G's wife walks alone around the wet, foggy streets of the town. She considers buying some Italian delicacies to take home but her heart isn't in it. She realises she doesn't actually believe in it any more, in reality – if Italy and its delicacies are reality. The thought makes her sad. Yet she has been so fortunate.

On the second day, in the afternoon, the sun unexpectedly advances from behind the clouds as though stepping through the curtain onstage. The world is transformed. G's wife is standing at that moment at the tall, heavy windows of their room which look out on the wet and desolate garden below. There has been very little she has found familiar here, from that other time so long ago. She recalls only blurred months of blazing heat and sun, full of sensuous pleasure and activity. This doleful return merely underscores the irretrievability of past time and the element of illusion, of belief, that she now sees constitutes so much of experience. She can't bear memory – she wants not to remember but to live and feel. If there were some way of erasing all her memories she would take it. Almost in the same moment that the sun bursts out she hears the sound of chatter and of doors banging down below and sees a family erupt onto the lawn. Her understanding of this sequence of events is far deeper than memory: it is a kind of creativity that applies knowledge to the ongoing moment. There are three small children – a girl and two boys – who speed all together across the lawn and a young father following more slowly behind them. They have obviously been glued to the windows waiting for the rain to stop. In the fresh sunlight the sudden greens of the garden are like a pulsing hallucination. Birds flit joyfully from tree to lawn and the flowers seem almost to lift up their heads and silently sing in the radiance. Her memories, also, are instantly illuminated: in fact the sunny garden and the children at play are so real to her that they bypass memory and hint at actual recurrence. She is once more in the garden entertaining her children while her husband works in a studio somewhere deep inside the cool and echoing villa. Her life is one of a continuous but diffuse momentum, like that of an ocean liner crossing seas with no visible landmark by which to gauge its progress. The movement, the progressing vessel, is her husband, and it has been easy, yes, easy and frequently scenic, absorbingly so, just as it is for the passengers on the ship's deck watching the sun rise and set over the water, seeing new colours and lights at the world's rim with an exalting sense of privilege at their witnessing of these things, then at other times weeks of storm and rain when they huddle inside and amuse themselves.

Down on the lawn the children's father is showing them something, kneeling while they gather round – an interesting flower or insect, perhaps. He is attractive squatting there in his loose jeans, slim and rugged-looking. She wonders how he manages to do his work and still have time for the children, as G never did. But G is a genius, and his selfishness may be one reason for it. Or perhaps the man's wife is the artist and he takes the female role. At the thought of this hypothetical woman she experiences terror, as if at the prospect of an ominous responsibility being thrust toward her. She imagines the woman in her studio, captaining the vessel as it plunges heedlessly forward.

Sometimes, at moments of crisis, she simply inverts her surroundings and instantly feels a sensation of peace. It is a habit she has got into over the years. Whatever is threatening or overwhelming in a set of circumstances is neutralised by being imagined upside down. It is the problem of perception, she understands, that has been removed – her implication in events is taken away. She is certain that G would not like to know this is what she does. Nevertheless she revolves the garden so that the brilliant green grass becomes the sky and the sky – so oblivious – tumbles with its fathomless blues and its cloud shapes to the earth. The heavy cypresses and the oaks hang from above, delirious with lightness. The man and the children are now just a patch of colour and texture among the other colours and textures, the burden of their humanity extinguished.

One day in an exhibition I saw a painting by the Black artist G of a cathedral, and for a long time afterward the memory of it stood in my mind. Sometimes I searched for photographs of it and looked at them and they resembled the memory but were not the same as it. They were photographs of the memory. The painting itself still existed somewhere, in time.

It had struck me as small, for the reason perhaps that its subject was big. By painting a small picture of a cathedral, G appeared to be making a comment about marginality. In the eye of this beholder, the grandiosity of man was thwarted: his products could be no bigger than he was himself. What was absent from the painting was any belief in what the cathedral was. I remembered it as resembling a glowing pile of blackened embers, charged with internal heat: it seemed to belong more to nature than to man. I wondered how this same artist might have painted a mountain. The justice he brought to the cathedral was of a rare kind, was something akin to love, or pity. He would not, perhaps, have pitied a mountain in the same way.

The reality or otherwise of monuments was a form of distraction in the cathedral painting, a facade behind which lay a relationship to power so oblique as to be almost ungraspable. It could perhaps be summed up as the idea that to stop experiencing the feeling of injustice would be to make the injustice no longer exist. It seemed to me that G liked the cathedral during the time that he looked at it, liked the way the sun made fire in its coloured windows so that the structure fell away into charred integuments. His liking was stronger than the cathedral, was more modern and alive. He chose to ignore the cathedral's power, like someone meeting a king and treating him as an equal, an instinctive though perilous kind of good manners.

I found out that G was one of very few Black painters in his circle, and he was excluded from most of its exhibitions and galleries. His work was appreciated but he was accorded no significance. It was exhibited after his death alongside that of certain female contemporaries, as though marginality were itself an identity, inalterable and therefore situated beyond change. The marginal becomes the central only later on, after the wars of ego have been fought, like a peacemaker arriving at the battlefield after the conflict has ended. G came to believe that art was useless as a tool of political change. Instead he exercised the right of the individual to seek aesthetic justification, a kind of morality for its own sake.

One day, in a museum, I unexpectedly saw the cathedral painting again. It was the school holidays and the museum was providing special activities for children. Entertainers in animal costumes were milling about the main hall, where music was playing and a disco ball suspended from the ceiling whirled coloured lights across

the walls. The children ran around directionlessly, screaming and laughing amid the discarded activity sheets
and the smells of food from the cafeteria. There was a
mild sensation of pandemonium, of a substanceless kind
of anarchy, like people misbehaving in church. But this
church of art was too fragile in its sanctity – its core of
belief was too menaced and lost – for it to bear much
public iconoclasm. The moral good of culture and the
values of entertainment were already locked in a dance
of death and needed no further encouragement. I was
thinking of the virtues of difficulty and of how people
who can find no reflection of themselves in their own circumstances might require proof of some boundlessness
to the human soul, some distant and inaccessible goal
toward which it reaches – might need to see the record
of those attempts and to realise how far people have
been prepared to run the risk of not being understood in
making them. Not to be understood is effectively to be
silenced, but not understanding can in its turn legitimise
that silence, can illuminate one's own unknowability. Art
is the pact of individuals denying society the last word.
There in the commotion of the museum I thought of G,
and of how as a child he had learned to draw by copying
pictures in books borrowed from the library in Harlem.
His neighbourhood later became his subject because it
was the subject that was given to him. The marginalised

41

artist, like any marginalised person, is obliged to reckon with reality first. But G eventually and deliberately set reality aside. Was abstraction – like imagination or fantasy – merely a mechanism of escape? Was there some debt that was left unpaid in this abandonment of the scene of limitation? It was a question not just about the moral value of freedom in the context of aestheticism, but about the actual nature of freedom itself.

Being hit in the head, I now saw, had been both real and unknowable, was the inversion of representation while being ultimately representative. The world is upside down, a friend of mine said when I told her what had happened to me. Yet the reality of violence, painful though it was, seemed to offer a correction to the reality that obeys the laws of gravity. What it offered was a bloody kind of truth. *You*, I called her, the woman who had hit me – called her in my mind, the hundreds of times I thought of her each day. She had replaced my image of myself, the image I had left behind me in the gilded mirror of the lady's apartment. She was my dark twin, the inextinguishable reminder of something that had been denied existence in myself. She herself did not deny it: her body was the entire limit of her being and she had chosen to deploy her objectification. She had done her work without making a sound. These were her offerings, the offerings of the stuntman: violence and silence.

In the museum I walked through the rooms at random, trying to escape the noise. In a large, long gallery where the paintings had been hung one above the other almost to ceiling height I suddenly saw it, the small smouldering canvas. It was somewhat lost among other, larger works and too far up the wall to properly see. It needed intimacy and proximity; it needed attention. Even here, in the safety of the museum, there was always this obligation, this fight to find a way out of obscurity. By that fact alone one might have said that G had failed to overcome his circumstances and attain a creative equality. In a sense the painting was a painting of that same failure. It was this, I realised, this summoning of the obscurity itself, that was so moving. It was his portion – it was what he had. He chose to represent it so as not to add more to the balance sheet of lost things: he was placing it on the scales of justice, this account of his refusal to be divided from himself. By painting the obscurity he is trying not to become angry with it. Instead he is trying to love it, the darkness in which he moves, the light that sometimes pierces it and that only his eyes can see.

The Midwife

It was well known that G's early years in the city had been wild. As time went by her circumstances had become more conventional, which everyone except her seemed to regard as a natural progression. Great success had come to her, and with it a husband and child, and money that needed to be converted into material things. Her wild years were safely behind her: it was apparently only she who had thought that things could go on as they were. But instead the wildness had become historic, and was now a certified source of allusion in her work, as foreign landscapes and exotic paraphernalia were in the works of the masters.

She lived with the husband and child and the child's nanny in a large house in a fashionable neighbourhood, and they also owned a place in the countryside not far from country places owned by people they knew. An architect had designed the country place for them, and it sometimes felt as though they were inhabiting his notion of how they should spend their time. There was a kitchen the size of a ballroom with a battalion of gleaming implements, and there was of course no ballroom, only an enormous white room with white sofas, like a polar landscape in which to entertain their friends. There was a studio he had designed for her adjacent to the house, facing not the valley that plunged down in great leaping mist-wreathed swathes of green, but the manicured garden, where it was expected that their child would play. He had installed tall windows all along this side of the studio, so that she would be able to see what the child was doing at every moment.

There were framed photographs on the walls of both houses, amidst pieces from their art collection and works by G herself. The photographer was G's husband. He had the images printed on thick white paper and framed at an exclusive place in the city. He described himself, in company, as an amateur. Most of the photographs were of their daughter. Everyone commented on what a beautiful child she was and the photographs confirmed this, while at the same time releasing her beauty out into the world like something too defenceless to survive there. Whenever G looked at the photographs she saw it, this bungled exposure, which revealed the feelings of the photographer as though they belonged to everybody, so that the child belonged to everybody too. The child never smiled in these photographs: nobody had told her to. She simply looked at the lens, her cherub's lips slightly parted, her round long-lashed eyes unwavering. Her composure was striking: it was easy to forget that what she was seeing was her father looking at her. Other people had photographs of their children blowing out birthday candles or playing football, but G's husband never photographed their daughter doing such things. It might have been that he wasn't interested in her on these occasions. The photographs required an act of participation that was also a form of submission: her distraction was not permitted. Over time G noticed something changing in the photographs of her daughter, because as the child came to realise she was being observed her submission became more visible.

G's studio in the city was situated in a dirty and dangerous neighbourhood, and she had so far fought off every pressure to move to more impressive premises. She herself did not fully know why this was. She was often frightened and uncomfortable in her studio. Far less successful artists had giant spaces in central locations where they received journalists and collectors, and even had exquisite meals delivered to these studios by their galleries. G thought that perhaps it was to demonstrate her disdain for these artists that she travelled across the city every day to her run-down quarters, and enjoyed the inconvenience suffered by those forced to seek her out. The studio in the city was the theatre of her wild years, when she used to sleep there on a mattress on the ground, surrounded by her easels and her materials. She was twenty-two years old and had run away from her parents and her own country. At some point her passport had disappeared into the studio's extraordinary disorder, never to be found again. She would call her parents from a vile-smelling callbox on the corner. She had told them she was studying in the city, but she was not a good liar. She kept forgetting the lie, and they would grow angered and disturbed by her incoherence. She would always remember how their disapproval made its way across hundreds of miles of land and sea and came into her twenty-two-year-old ear down the filthy cord of that phone on the corner of her street. Once, on the way back from the callbox, a madman chased her and she had to run into her building and slam the door in his face.

The way her parents had combined authority with neglect had made it impossible for her to free herself from them. Since childhood her attempts to appease their authority had contorted her whole being, but she had transformed their neglect into something she herself was barely able to grasp, a violent power that remained unknowable even as it surged out of her, waking her up early in the morning and directing her mechanically to her easel. There was no mirror in the studio then, or maybe she just didn't think to look at herself. Her memory of that time was of a complete erasure or absence of an exterior self. Her body was simply a method for making her conceptions into material objects.

Other people she knew were helped or given money by their families, but her dependence on her parents seemed to be increased by their refusal to give her these things. Once she had succeeded in moving geographically away from them she could easily have cut herself off from them completely, but instead she went diligently to the callbox to expose herself to their disapproval. It was obvious that she disgusted them, yet she still hoped to win their love – and this was the curious part – by doing things that could only disgust them more. Their disapproval, in other words, never succeeded in obstructing her will, however much she might have wanted it to be obstructed. Her parents were disturbed by her painting and threatened by its candour and so she became more candid still, as though the problem arose from the fact that she had not yet given a sufficiently thorough explanation of herself. Their disapproval tended to converge around the same themes as the salient instincts of her talent, and by this means she knew herself to be drawing closer to the truth. It was glorious to feel the resilience of her art, its immunity not just against the opinions of others but against her own errant psychology. Over time a line, or was it a wall, had begun to divide her work from her self. But back in the wild years that line did not yet exist. She was one riotous disorderly kingdom, bankrupt, continually menaced, but not yet invaded.

She had worked in a bar and slept on the mattress on the floor and barely managed to feed and wash herself. No one had ever taught her how to treat herself with care. The other people who lived like that were all boys. She never met a girl who didn't wash her hair and put on clean clothes and remove her make-up before getting into bed. Some of the boys she slept with found her disgusting, as her parents had. They were rude and ungentlemanly. The girls were also rude, mocking the thick powder she wore to cover up her bad skin and the clumsy way she put on her signal-red lipstick. She found that when she had sex she could be free for a while from her hatred of her body, but she had to overcome her fear of disgust first. She painted frenziedly but with no clear goal, until one day a boy who was hanging around her studio mentioned that his parents owned an art gallery. She didn't really know what an art gallery was, though afterward no one ever believed this to be true. The galleries she knew about were public museums, where she spent her time studying certain paintings and then trying to surmount their influence in her studio. It had never occurred to her that what she was doing bore any concrete relationship to these paintings. Yet some weeks later she went to the boy's parents' gallery with a portfolio of her work. Her memory of this period was both keen and opaque, dazzlingly strange, the magnificent intrusion into her private world like footprints in virgin snow. Later she saw it as simply another example of the way her painting functioned autonomously, living in her like some organism that had happened to make its home there. It had never failed to sustain itself.

She stayed with the boy's parents' gallery for three years, and began to make enough money to give up the job in the bar. She went to openings at other galleries and met other artists. Something had changed: somehow she had become identifiably female. This was not a sexual but a social femininity, offered to her as a form of weakness. It entailed judgement, not of her person but of her actions. Her actions were chaotic and lacked self-interest. She sometimes felt other people looking out at her from within their own self-interest, puzzled or amused. She felt gaudy and exposed, and when she looked back on this time now – now that composure was finally within her grasp, whether or not she troubled to reach for it – she was swept by a terrible grief, for it was in that provisional, perilous and occasionally thrilling period while she thrashed the work out of her body that she understood she had been unloved. At an opening she met the owner of a small new gallery, who asked to visit her studio the next day. He was a funny little man, ugly and sweet-natured, and something mongrel about him legitimised her own ugliness, so that in his presence she felt seen as though in a strong and neutral north light. In the years that followed they made fame for one another, for he had the gift of turning her persona inside out so that suddenly she made sense. What felt like her unacceptability became, when it was externalised, something unassailably objective.

These days her gallerist was a slim, cold, effective character with a handsome chiselled face and impeccably ironed clothes. When she had discovered his age – he was ten years younger than her – she had felt a quiet dismay. She had grown used to her own precocity, which had always guaranteed that she was younger than everyone else around her. He had small children, and they talked about parenthood, sitting in her studio in the country house where her daughter and her daughter's nanny could often be seen through the windows. His stories about his children were thoughtful and amusing – he was a very clever man, after all – but she noticed that they always ended well, with no ragged edge of doubt or failure around them. His spotless clothes and his unhurried manner suggested another plane on which parenthood was a reasonable, well-planned and enjoyable event. In the garden her daughter and the nanny always looked as though they were waiting for something, like an audience waiting for the play to start. In a way it was a triumph of civilisation, that she and the gallerist could sit in the calm, coherent light of her studio and discuss their children, without either of them having to do anything about them. The conversation moved easily on to her work and to whatever new and prestigious opportunity he had secured for her. A bolt of terror would sometimes fly through her heart then, as he delicately steered her back to the business at hand, and she felt the desire to rush out of the studio door into the garden and pick up her daughter and run with her, run out of the gates as fast as she could and away up the road.

In need of escape, we sometimes went to Mann's farm, where a cottage was rented out in the grounds of the property. The cottage was at the top of a steep valley that plunged down to the sea. The valley was covered with green scrub and thorn bushes and olive trees, and far at the bottom a plain of reed beds undulated beside a glittering inlet. It looked as though it was possible to walk directly from the cottage down to the water, but beyond the farm the thick, dry vegetation was impenetrable. An extensive network of wire fences demarcated the uncultivated terrain. Mann's wife told us that these parcels of apparently useless land had been carefully marked out by their owners, in anticipation of a time when the regulations would be lifted and the land could be built on, as had happened elsewhere on the island.

The few paths were meandering and indirect and rarely led to what could be seen most obviously ahead. They travelled off aimlessly or secretively elsewhere. There was mystery in the winding shadows of the wooded ravines and in the rippling reed beds on the plains beside the sea, and up on the hills the obscure forms of giant white boulders seemed to stare out at the piercing blue water. Behind them rose the mountain, with its jagged white head flung madly into the sky. Its white-and-silver surfaces stood bare and unassailable, the colossal shape not sloping but cuboid, composed of innumerable facets that flashed from its sides in the sun. There was something diabolical and machine-like in these glinting rectilinear faces. The little potholed road down to the sea trailed distractedly away across the hillside and into the next valley, winding and winding downward through clefts of forested emptiness. Goats stood motionless in the contorted boughs of the olive trees amid the shrieking of cicadas. The reeds made a hissing sound as the winds surged through them. The shrill heat scoured the land and sky and rendered them senseless, and always in the distance was the illegible mountain, whose violent authority could be seen from everywhere.

At the entrance to Mann's property were a pair of large wrought-iron gates, dilapidated now, that had been fabricated in a pattern of arcane geometric shapes and symbols framing the letters of his name. A rough track led to the house, through dusty fields strewn with rusting machinery and piles of wood and evidence of projects started then abandoned. A herd of shaggy brown cattle with giant heads and huge horns like staves roamed freely across the fallen fences among the olive trees and in the shade of the copses, where two or three old caravans stood in a clearing. Around the house was a farmyard, filled with squabbling geese and chickens and a number of tiny black pigs, who tumbled riotously in the dust and chased the kittens who sometimes leaped down from the low garden wall to provoke them. The farmyard was well kept, with tubs of nasturtiums and vines climbing over the roofs of the hutches, and Mann's wife was often to be seen there, tending to the animals.

The farmhouse was a stone structure with no obvious entrance, for it was clad in an incomprehensible patch-work of wooden lean-tos and additions, all splintered and faded by the sun. The first time we went there, not knowing how to announce ourselves, we stood and waited outside in the farmyard, where a slim black dog came to greet us. Presently the dog trotted inside, through a small door that stood ajar at the side of the building.

Shortly afterward Mann's wife came out, and we were to learn that the dog would always go to find her if she was needed. She showed us to the cottage, which was some way from the farmhouse across the dusty fields, facing out over the valley. Enormous cacti grew there, with thick curving arms that reached out and toppled to the ground, where they continued to wind across the earth like snakes, and in the dusk their strange forms converged so that they resembled that of a mythological creature. In the distance, on the opposite ridge, a quarry could faintly be seen lying like an earth-coloured scar across the green.

The cottage was functional and plain, and its furnishings old and outdated, but like the farmyard it was orderly and homelike, and this evidence of good housekeeping seemed to stand in opposition to the spirit of chaos that presided elsewhere on the farm. Mann's wife was small and sturdy, with a braid of chestnut hair and small eyes whose fierce blue pupils looked out keenly and in some puzzlement from her bronzed face, as though she had been misled and was now determined to see the truth of what was in front of her. She invited us to come to the house whenever we wished so that she could supply us with eggs and vegetables from her garden, and she taught us how to secure the rickety gate to stop the cows from breaking in.

There was a man called Johann living in one of the caravans in the clearing, and sometimes we stopped to talk
to him. He was a schoolteacher from Germany, a friend
of Mann's wife, and he told us that every year he came to
the farm for a few months to help her with the livestock
and with producing the oil and wine. His encampment
was very organised and neat, and he had even made a
small garden where flowers and vegetables grew in hoed
rows. This place is falling apart, he said, but I do what I
can. Twenty years ago it was paradise here, he said, and
it would still be that way in my mind if I never came back,
and spent my holidays at the beach like everyone else.
He told us that at one time this farm had been a myth-
ical place, where people could come and join Mann's
community and receive the basic necessities for living in
return for labour. Mann had stumbled by chance on the
valley, which had remained more or less untouched by
the modern era, and had bought the land and the farm
for next to nothing. His idea had been to create a society
that was entirely self-sufficient and had no need of the
world. He had decided to try to stop time here, because
it was the most beautiful place he had ever seen.

It was like a beautiful innocent girl, Johann said drily,
who he wanted to stay a virgin forever.

The people who came were young, and couldn't see
anything worthwhile in the boring German cities where

they lived, though they all went back to those cities in the end, Johann said, and got jobs and bought expensive cars, and now if they came to the island it was for their summer holiday. A lot of people came, he said, but Mann's wife was the only one who stayed.

He told us that Mann had fought for years to keep development out of the valley, and had become so deeply enmeshed in local politics that over time the farm had fallen into decay. He's spent so much time with corrupt officials, Johann said with some disgust, that he's turned the same colour as them, and even if you think his cause is just, the issues of power and domination start to look the same from both sides. The difference is that Mann doesn't understand money, he said, but he needs it just like everyone else does. He's tied himself up in so many complicated deals that they can never be unravelled. This farm has a bad case of woodworm, he said significantly. It's been hollowed out just as men always hollow things out. The only money it makes is what she can get from the cottage.

At the farmhouse the small side door stood ajar, and when we knocked and received no response we simply pushed it open and went in. We entered a large, high-ceilinged room in a state of astonishing disorder, where books and papers were stacked into precarious towers on every surface and rusted or broken equipment lay everywhere, along with tattered clothes, old shoes, empty bottles and armchairs disgorging their stuffing. On a large desk in the middle stood what appeared to be a giant radio, in a tangle of wires and antennae. A thick sediment of dust lay over everything. There were tall windows all along one side through which a light at once clear and diffuse, like that of a church, streamed over the chaotic scene. The sound of women's voices could be heard somewhere nearby and we followed it, passing along a low passageway that led into a large, old-fashioned kitchen with a gleaming stone floor and a shining copper cauldron hanging in the fireplace.

Mann's wife stood by the window, with a young girl and a tiny old woman dressed in black with a black scarf on her head. The three of them looked up when we entered and immediately fell silent. In the silence the triangle of their three faces bore an aspect of conspiracy. Mann's wife introduced the young girl as her daughter, while the old woman went and busied herself at the sink, where a basket of vegetables stood. The girl was very small and pale, with long black hair and large glasses through which her brown eyes peered slightly dolefully. But when she spoke it was with a shy smile, and her eyes didn't look away. We were invited to sit at the scrubbed-wood table while our provisions were prepared. Mann's wife asked us questions and the girl listened attentively to the answers.

The kitchen was as clean and orderly as the other room had been dusty and chaotic. The tiny old woman smiled to herself as she worked, her brown face deeply grooved with wrinkles. Our provisions were packed into a basket and Mann's wife accompanied us back through the house to the door.

This is my husband's room, she said when we came to the high-ceilinged space with its bedlam of disorder and filth. The light fell on the thick layer of dust so that it resembled snow. I'm not allowed to interfere with anything here, she said, her eyes assuming their puzzled expression. It's the kitchen that belongs to me. He made that himself, she added, pointing to the radio. He talks on it to people all over the world. He speaks five languages, she said, and he likes to keep them up. It's obviously very impressive, she said, but I admit that sometimes I ask myself what use five languages are on a farm.

She told us about a route to get to the sea by foot, and the next day we walked down there. The path descended steeply across a barren hillside that bulged out over the water like a giant's forehead, and a feeling arose that we were to have often in that place, that we were being watched. It was not a human or animal scrutiny that we felt upon us. Rather, it was the land itself that seemed to possess some ambiguous spirit of observation. Rearing overhead was the mountain, at once crystalline and obscure in the last light, and it did feel as though this ghostly gathering of information was directed there, to the increase of its mute and basking form. In the blind monomaniacal eyes of that mountain, to be human was a pitiable, if not an incomprehensible fate.

Shame had always stood behind G, colossal and constrained, like water behind a dam. In the early days her studio in the city was a place of shamelessness where she could forget this silent presence behind her, but one day – whether out of curiosity or impatience – she decided to acknowledge it. She began a series of paintings in which her sense of shame was permitted to guide the evolution of the image. G thought of these vaguely as autobiographical paintings. There was a running impulse somewhere in her work, as though she were constantly fleeing or pursuing or proving something, as though she was always climbing mountains, and it was this feeling of exertion, or compulsion, that she suddenly wanted no more of. The word she found for it was shame. This word made her stop and look around herself.

G decided that shame emanated from the body and was not the same as regret or embarrassment. It was not conscious or analytical. It was associated with production, with the body as a product and the body's own products. It would have been much easier to express this in a three-dimensional form and people were, G knew, expressing it that way. But a form could only correspond – it couldn't smash anything or break it down. A form utilised silence, when what G wanted was disclosure. She wanted to speak, to tell. This telling seemed to relate to childhood and so she made some childhood paintings. They were rather horrible, pornographic and gleeful, but she felt something moving volcanically underneath them, as though the whole surface were about to crack open and erupt. She was no longer running up and down mountains and exhausting herself. She was offering her products, as though with a sickening smile.

G forgot that people would have to look at the paintings. She painted everything she dreaded and hated, but joyously, like a child exerting power in private by playing with plastic figures and making them do things to each other. What this lacked was precision, devastation. How could she impose precision on shame? The narratives shame produced were usually labours of imagination that resulted in fantasy or pornography. She didn't want to imagine – she wanted to name. G painted a portrait of a woman, using photographs. The photographs were from a magazine she had found, that dated from the era of her childhood. They showed the woman in numerous poses on a leopard-skin rug. They were outdated and lush, glamour shots, mildly pornographic. She remembered seeing such things at the time and the particular kind of alarm they had caused her. Her girlhood, which she still held like an unopened letter, had recoiled from them as though from news of a conspiracy – a conspiracy past, present and future – not just among these docile, compliant women but between them and the image-maker. Why had no one intervened in this horror taking place between the photographer and the woman on the leopard-skin rug? G hated photographers, those cowardly voyeurs. And she hated this woman in the photograph, whom she feared and blamed in equal measure, blamed historically, because someone had to take responsibility for the dirty pact of history, which denied any difference between her image and her being. It was through her complicity that the terms of G's own exclusion from the image were constituted. Her complicity sent G into exile and forced her to conceal herself. It was what made G aberrant and unacceptable – it was what made all women non-artists. G painted several portraits of this woman, and came to feel that she had murdered and replaced the photographer, and perhaps even atoned for him. Eventually she stopped being angry with the woman too, and decided to love her. She lavished attention on her, which made her feel better, and when she realised that the woman in the photographs would actually be quite old by now she began carefully to break her down and return her to colour and light and non-being.

G kept to this diffuse mode of perception, using it to describe the history of her sexual encounters and finding that she was free of shame, that her sexual memory could become a pagan kind of pastoral, an orgiastic panorama full of heavenly colours. Her technical competence, rather than exhausting itself with feats of representation or satire, put itself at the service of internal self-description, and the accuracy she was able to achieve through the discipline of candour was remarkable. However bizarre and inadmissible she found her own ideas, the way they functioned as truth was startling. The ugly, sweet-natured gallerist watched these developments with serene satisfaction, and she never told him that she had expected him to drop her when he saw the new work, because the idea of it making sense to anyone other than herself had been unimaginable. One day he said that he thought it was time G had a show, and he began to spread word of her recent activities in the shambling, diffident way he had that focused, ambitious people found so irresistible.

It was at this time that G met her husband. Someone – a critic – had asked G at a party whether she was in a strong relationship and said that he hoped that she was, because the degree of attention she was about to receive might be somewhat destabilising for a young woman. G remembered thinking that what she in fact wanted was to be destabilised, but this warning must have alerted her in some deeper way, because by her second or third encounter with her husband she was ready to come out, like the cornered suspect in a film, with her hands up. He was a lawyer, a friend of somebody who had brought him along to the opening of her show, and he had wandered around for a long time not talking to anyone and looking at the paintings. His self-containment and solitude had caught her eye, but it was his disapproval that seduced her. She recognised in his disapproval the mark of authority. While claiming to know nothing about art, which at a stroke seemed both to diminish her achievements and to increase his air of importance, he gave G to understand that there was something morally repellent in her work that she was perhaps unaware of. The show was an extraordinary critical success, but for him this was merely proof that people were mindlessly feasting on her self-exposure. G had got out of the habit of recognising authority and so she gave it a joyous welcome. The sound of his disapproval was that of something long-lost but familiar. Later it was he who wished to put the wild years into a historical context, especially once he had seen how profitable they were, but at the beginning his disgust encompassed not only her work but her self, or rather treated them as the same thing. Like a dog slinking back to a cruel master, she came at the call of his disgust, much as she had gone diligently to the callbox on the corner to receive it from across land and sea into her ear.

A time of great restructuring and reorganisation followed. G moved into this man's apartment and adapted to his way of living, which was much more bourgeois than her own. It was the life, or so she thought, of an adult. When he was at work she would go from room to room in the sunlight, touching his things. She was jealous of his former girlfriend, who was more beautiful than G and who she feared he still loved. Each time they spent an evening with people she knew, he would produce afterward a detailed indictment of their characters and conduct, and she discovered that she no longer liked them as much as she once had. She became more solitary and less friendly, and lost her feeling of camaraderie with artists of her own age. Her gallerist was silent on the subject of G's husband, and his silence seemed to contain something of herself, something ominous that was related to betrayal: when he looked at G, it was as though he was remembering a person G had mistreated. Slowly G found herself withdrawing from her gallerist: their relationship acquired a new distance and formality. Her husband was in the habit of making pointed observations about the gallerist's treatment of her, and of highlighting the ways in which other artists were more respected and recognised than she. The days when he claimed to know nothing about art were far behind him. He had mastered her life as he would have a legal brief. For the first time G found herself misreading situations and even sometimes coming into conflict with people. She felt embattled and exposed.

Yet her paintings were making money and her reputation was in rapid ascent. She forgot that the reasons for this lay in the work she had done before she met her husband, and attributed her new-found security to him. Her work became sombre and more formally beautiful. She painted a number of big oils that showed a seamless, almost featureless surface, quietly undulating like the surface of the sea. They seemed to hang mutely and pacifically between death and life. They proposed something non-human, a spiritual quest. G had never even considered having a child, but now she considered it. Once, when she was younger, she had discovered she was pregnant – she didn't know by whom – and had had an abortion without hesitation or emotion. She had despised the idea of feeling emotion about something so rational. She had rid her body of an intruder as she might have shooed a bird out of a room. When she told her husband this, he looked at her with distaste. That's very sad, he said. Was it sad? G considered the blank, mechanical space where her sadness ought to have been. She was filled suddenly with the terror of being unloved. She imagined the hypothetical baby, the one she had shooed away. A chasm of horror seemed to open up beneath her. She realised that she was monstrous, a monster of moral indifference. Would her husband consider redeeming her by giving her his child? He didn't seem all that keen on the idea – after all, she wasn't to be trusted in this area. But eventually he allowed himself to be persuaded.

G got through pregnancy awkwardly and with embarrassment. The people in her world also seemed embarrassed – what was this rude biological bulk she was imposing on them and on their sensibilities? Her loyalty wavered as a dreadful truth, the truth of her female caste, came slowly and inexorably into view, with its smouldering fires of injustice and servitude. She was toying, she saw, with inferiority, and she regarded the clean-cut bodies of men in terror, hating them while wanting to retain kinship with them. The baby was a girl, a result G immediately viewed as a failure. She had wanted and expected her body to produce the prestige of masculinity. But this girl very quickly brought light to G, a light like the dawn of the world, fresh and clear and revelatory. Everything outside this light was sickening and corrupt, but within its circle was a secret. G and the baby shared this secret. The only problem was the baby's body, which had to be continually cared for by G and taken with her everywhere. She often wished they could share a body, as they had when she was pregnant. But then again, by being born the girl had returned G to herself. It was this return, with its increase in the form of the girl, that was revelatory. G wanted to run away with her, but the problem of the baby's body and who it belonged to prevented her. She identified the baby with everything that was true about herself and with the secret they shared. Her power of sight was doubled, now that the baby's perspective was added to it: she started to see good and evil in what had up until now been the pressing disorder of reality. She started to see her husband more clearly, without the illusion of love. One night they argued horribly, frighteningly, and she took the baby and went to sleep in another room. This was the first time she had fulfilled her urge to run away with the baby, and as she lay beside her in the darkness, lacerated, she felt bathed in a feeling of comfort and peace such as she had never known. A few minutes later the door opened and she saw her husband's silhouette in the frame. He looked at the two of them lying there, and then he advanced briskly into the room, picked up the baby, and took her away, closing the door firmly behind him.

There was nothing for G to do but return to her studio

and work. She hired a nanny to look after the baby. The nanny was her drudge, her alter ego, her shame. G worked strongly, filled with competence and rage. Often when she returned from work her husband was already there, with the nanny and their daughter. He had a little pursed look of reproach about him as he did things for the child, even though G was paying the nanny to do those things. He had taken to spending more time at home, and she understood that this was because he was not going to allow her to take possession of their daughter. Over time she came to feel that it was because her love was defective and because she herself did not want to be at home. The nanny adored the husband: it was apparently miraculous to see a man caring for his own child. The three of them were usually in the kitchen, which somehow had become the venue for the demonstration of their life, like a theatre where they enacted their roles. There was always a moment, as she came in, when they fell silent and their three faces would look up. More and more, as time passed, her daughter's face seemed to look at her across some unbreachable distance, as at something she no longer knew but remembered.

The days passed slowly and indistinguishably at Mann's farm, as though they were the same day examined from different angles, like the sparkling facets of a diamond.

The sky was pink at dawn and the great mop-like shapes of the many-armed cacti lay slumbering in the garden in the new light. Slowly the sun awakened the empty valley, pushing back the curtain of shadow from its forested slopes and its reed beds and its vegetation like tangled hair. The ochre wound of the quarry glittered when the sun touched it and the sound of birdsong and of the cattle rustling in the dry olive groves began to infiltrate the waiting silence. We walked down to the water along the path, scattering the goats who scrambled away with their clattering bells, the steep and rocky descent turning and turning above the sea. There was an abandoned house there on the hillside, up a track that turned off the path, whose red roof could be glimpsed among the canopies of the olive trees. One day we went to look at it, as though lured by its human correspondence with ourselves. It was a long, low building in a desolate clearing, painted stark white with windows that stared straight out to the sea. Behind it stood the mountain, pyramidal and somehow malign, as though it were laughing at this evidence of failure, for in places the roof had fallen in and there were goats hopping among the ruins of the outbuildings. Through the windows the rooms could be seen, still furnished, the pots and pans on the kitchen shelves, a chair drawn up to the blackened fireplace, a coat hanging on a hook and a newspaper lying open on the dining table, as though the occupants had simply vanished.

One afternoon, passing the farmhouse on our way to the cottage, we saw a man standing in the yard. He was very tall and emaciated, with long wild white hair and a long and filthy white beard, and his thin parted lips disclosed the fact that several of his yellow teeth were missing. He wore no shoes and his clothes were little more than dirty rags. He looked at us with a confused half-grin, as though uncertain of who and where he was. A horrible stain trailed down his beard and across his puny chest. Just then Mann's wife came out of the farmhouse, with the dog at her heels. She said something to the man, an expression of impatience on her face, and he turned away from her imperiously, lifting his head as though listening to a sound in the distance. When she noticed us standing there she came across to talk to us. The man still looked off into the air like a distracted prophet, appearing not to notice, but then shortly afterward he followed her over, as though he had decided to do so of his own accord.

This is Mann, she said. This is my husband.

It was a day of brutal heat. The valley below lay stunned, pulsing in the throbbing air. The cows stood with drooping heads beneath the olive trees. Mann's wife asked us whether it was too hot in the cottage, and offered to bring us an electric fan.

They shouldn't come here if they need to be cool, Mann said unexpectedly, in a high, clear, cultivated voice that was entirely incongruous with his wild appearance.

Mann's wife gave a derisive laugh.

It's too late, she said. They're already here.

He raised his hand, as though to silence her. He was so thin that the tendons on his dirty neck and arms bulged out beneath the skin.

In that case, he said, they should do as the animals do and stay still in the shade.

After the first shock of Mann's appearance, the lineaments of his face started to become clear. Beneath his matted hair and beard he had a high domed forehead and a fine, delicate nose. His cheekbones were wide and flat. His eyes were a strange pale green, and he held them open and unblinking as though in messianic rapture. Mann's wife looked at him with open contempt.

Not everyone wants to live like an animal, she said.

Mann turned his head slowly toward her, as though finally deciding to acknowledge her. There was something studied in this vagueness that suggested a formulated response to challenges to his authority.

Not everyone subscribes to bourgeois values as you do, he said.

Her face flushed a dark red and her eyes flashed.

There's nothing wrong with wanting a clean and

comfortable home, she said. Especially if there are children.

Mann jerked back his head with impatience.

Oh, children! he said sardonically. How many times have I heard them used as an excuse for abandoning principles?

The dog started to whine and Mann's wife laid her hand on its head.

Children have natural principles, she said hotly, and Mann parted his thin lips in a gasping laugh.

In that case, he said, they're the only beings who do.

Later that afternoon Mann's wife brought us the electric fan. The black dog leaped nimbly over the gate and trotted into the garden, and Mann's wife followed slowly after it. She was damp with sweat, and she sat with us for a while in the shade to cool down before her walk back to the house. She wore a faded lilac sundress that showed her strong brown shoulders and arms. Her keen blue eyes moved back and forth across the valley.

This is an ugly heat, she said, and it comes more and more.

The dog lay curled at her feet, its sides moving sharply in and out, but even in the heat it found it difficult to stay still, and at her every movement its head would shoot up, alert, and look around.

She asked us whether we had found the path down to

the sea, and we told her about the abandoned house we had seen, with its ghostly air of habitation. She told us that it had belonged to the same family for many years, but now the old parents had died and the children wanted to sell it. They had all left the island as soon as they could, she said, and never came back here, and their idea was to sell the house and land to a developer who might build a hotel. The position and the view of the sea were so exceptional that they'd put it on the market for a very high price, but each time a developer was interested the council rejected their application. The children are very angry, she said, but they are also very stubborn. They've decided to wait for their money because they believe that one day, when there are different people on the council, the application will be approved. They haven't touched the house, she said, which in their scheme would be demolished, and have left all their parents' things exactly as they were when they died. Their clothes are still in the cupboards and their toothbrushes in the bathroom and their packets of food on the shelves, and I often think about how those old people would feel, she said, to discover they had been left exposed in that way.

She apologised for her accent, which she knew she retained in spite of having lived here for longer than she'd lived in Germany.

I don't know why my accent sticks to me, she said. Like

the dog sticks to me. She's Mann's dog, she said, but she doesn't seem to know it.

She sat unselfconsciously with her brown legs planted apart and her elbows resting on the arms of her chair, and every now and again she pushed away the strands of her hair that had fallen over her forehead with a mechanical gesture.

My daughter has the same accent, she said, and she's been to Germany only a few times in her life. She doesn't feel at home in Germany, and nor do I any more. She was very ill as a child, she said, and my family couldn't believe that I didn't take her back there for treatment. For them a child's illness is a sign that it's time for you to stop running away and to go back to their reality. They think that a place like this isn't actually real, that people aren't born here, that they don't feel things and believe in their lives like people in Germany do. It's ironic, she said, because people here live much longer than they do there, so long that a lot of them don't even know how old they are. There are people here who remember snow on the mountain, she said. They remember a time when there were ghosts here, who were as real to them as they were to each other. Nothing is left of that time, she said, but it doesn't seem to make them sad. They may live long lives, she said, but their rapport with death has always seemed to me more intimate.

She began to talk about a tradition on the island – or perhaps, she said, it was just a myth – of a community figure who could be called upon to assist with death, rather as a midwife assists with birth. In fact she had been told that it was often the same person who did both. The assistance, in the case of death, was somewhat shocking: if a person decided it was time for them to die, this midwife would undertake the job in the swiftest and most efficient way possible. A single hammer blow to the head while the person was sleeping was the customary method, and she had seen what were purported to be these hammers – wooden, club-like objects that were often intricately carved – not just in the island museum but also in people's own homes. According to the myth, she said, the sign for this midwife of death to take action was when a person discreetly left their door ajar at night. It's hard not to think of the possibilities for error, she said, but I tend to think that this woman – and it is always a woman, apparently – is subtle enough to know when the message is for her.

Down below, at the foot of the simmering valley, speedboats were criss-crossing the flat surface of the sea, driving white furrows into the water. The sound of their engines and of voices crying out could faintly be heard. In the distance, on the opposite ridge, lay the quarry, where the tiny forms of diggers were moving mechanically and glinting in the sun. The effortless machines seemed to exist in a different reality from that of the hot hillside, with its primitive scene of human struggle.

He tried to stop that quarry, Mann's wife said. I forgot that you can still see it from here. Everywhere else he planted trees to block out the view. For him it was the beginning of the end, she said, when the quarry company came. He couldn't understand how the local people just seemed to accept it. He couldn't bear the sight of it so he planted trees, she said, and then he didn't have to look at it any more.

The dog raised its head and laid it on her knee and she pushed it gently away, fanning her face with her hand.

It's too hot, Lola, she said.

She wiped her forehead and stood up, and the dog leaped up and ran around her in circles. She told us that she would shortly be returning to Germany for a few days as her mother was ill. The housekeeper, Grazia – the tiny old woman we had seen – would help us with anything we needed. Her mother had been ill for a while, she said. There was nothing she could do for her, but the obligation couldn't be avoided: the family were always arguing about whose turn it was to visit her. It was such a contrast to the island, she said, where old people were beloved, that she had come to dread these encounters with her mother, because the cynicism of their familial bonds increasingly felt to her like something that needed to be confronted before it was too late. But as soon as she was there she immediately saw how impossible such a confrontation would be.

My mother doesn't understand my life, she said. She says that all I am is a workhorse. It seems strange for a mother to think that her child is a horse, she said, but the truth is often cruel in that way. Whenever I go back to Germany, she said, I feel as if I've woken up from a dream. Of course the reality of it has changed so much since I left, and I don't belong there any more, but it's also true that in a way I am living in a dream. I don't know anything there, she said, wrinkling her blue eyes in bewilderment, but here there's something I know.

G made friends with a woman painter her own age. She was not friends with many women. The painter said to her, me and you are the old guard, referring not just to their age but to their medium of paint, and G wanted to get away from her as fast as she could. The painter talked about her own body as though it had no secrets, and G realised that shame had stealthily taken her again in its grip. The cheerful way the painter spoke about their mutual redundancy struck G as disingenuous. But she never found any evidence to support that opinion.

G made a series of big erotic pictures in which she believed her own bitterness and constraint to be concealed. She appeared to be revelling in the freedom of the male body while in fact experiencing a horrible sensation of transference that almost amounted to hatred. She wondered if men had hated the nudes they painted in the same way. She stayed far away from reality, working from photographs. The paintings felt cynical to her, mendacious, but cynicism and mendacity were very popular, if her gallerist's response was anything to go by. She felt more inclined these days to believe what other people said about her work. In its autonomy it had opened up a more radical distance from her consciousness, where huge and increasingly nameless shapes drifted with a hulking, unbroachable violence.

She lived obediently in the bare routines of family life. When she met her male peers at parties or openings she saw them as free and herself as enchained. Even if they had families themselves she elaborated her story of their freedom. They were unscheduled, unhurried – they inhabited one glittering moment after another. She felt as if she was living in simultaneous realities, like the clocks in airports that showed the time in different cities across the world. The men looked her directly in the eye, as though to tell her how overjoyed they were to be integrated with their own bodies. They noticed her dislocation. They were clothed in self-interest. They looked at her with the same puzzlement she remembered from her youth.

The woman painter didn't go to these parties – she said she preferred to stay at home. She lived with her son in a warm, untidy house where people were always coming and going. She often painted random, unframed sections of this interior, as though she were an object blamelessly looking at other objects. These paintings reminded G of how her life used to feel and no longer did. They were curiously shocking, if only because they did not engage in the moral barter of representation. They made her own work seem exploitative and wilful. The painter was G's only female rival in success, yet there did not seem to be an actual rivalry between them. On the contrary, the painter treated her as an ally. She assumed a loyalty and kinship with G that G was not certain she herself felt. In the painter's studio, which was attached to her house and where her son ran in and out, G sometimes felt a suffocating sense of exile from everything that she valued. She felt stifled by the painter's femininity, her warmth and lack of aggression. The painter was as unhurried and unscheduled as a man, but in a different way. G wanted her to hurry, to flee from her own contentment and disorder, as though her lack of urgency was unwittingly condemning her to quicksands of female irrelevance.

The painter came to a dinner party at G's house. Dressed up, she seemed sensuous and beautiful. She looked at the lavish, sterile space. She looked at the photographs of G's daughter that hung everywhere. She wore an expression of interest tinged with amusement. G's husband treated her with the extreme courtesy that was the sign of his loathing. She stayed until long after midnight, drank wine and smoked several cigarettes, and when G's husband asked pointedly whether he could open the windows she looked at him with beautiful wide eyes and said, I don't care what you do. The painter visited G's studio in the city not long afterward. She took in the studio's filth and disorder and cleared a space for herself on one of the two available chairs. She gazed speculatively at the canvas on G's easel. What are you doing? she said.

G felt a larger interrogation behind this question, though the painter probably didn't mean it that way. People rarely interrogated or questioned her. Only her husband seemed to understand how willing she was to be interrogated and her actions condemned. The paintings in the studio were illicit attempts at communication behind the backs of the authority figures that had dogged her life. Her imagining of what lay beyond the parameters of authority had become too contorted and fevered, she saw. She was frightened and jealous and self-hating, and she had tried to disguise this by feigning intimacy with what she was frightened of. The painting on the easel was an ugly fantasy of others and their tormenting and threatening desires. G's husband no longer questioned her moral worth, in her art at least. He was entirely immersed in the money she made, and reserved his disapproval for her domestic persona. The fact that he took no notice of the ugly erotic paintings was the proof, G saw, of their weakness. In fact he liked them, because they were profitable and weak. There was something she could do that would shock him, because the judgement he incarnated was vulnerable to shock, but she didn't know what it was. Her ability to shock had always been instinctive and unconscious.

The painter, only half-joking, asked G whether she was living a double life, and G remembered the evening of the dinner party, when she had suddenly felt her conventionality on humiliating display. The painter had seen it all, she knew, and G wanted to protest that she hadn't chosen what the painter saw, but the fact was that she had. She had chosen it, had sometimes even forced it to be. What she wanted was for someone to ask her why she had, to see through her as her husband did but from the other side of the mirror. The painter asked her where her daughter was in the paintings. G felt a lurching motion beneath her at this question, as though she were on a suddenly listing boat. The inescapability of her life shrank in an instant to this small and unstable boat. Obviously, the painter said, before G could say it herself, I wouldn't ask that question to a man.

Around this time G's husband received the news that his father was dying, on the other side of the country. His mother asked him to come and help her but he refused to go. He explained to his mother that he couldn't simply abandon his responsibilities in that way: she would have to manage on her own. G listened to her husband talking on the phone to his mother. She could hear her weeping while he upbraided her – he often upbraided G in precisely this way. He sounded reasonable and extremely important, but the woman's tinny cries down the receiver supplied a new dimension of horror to G's ears. Then the mother had a stroke and had to be taken to hospital, and so there was no choice but for G's husband to go – with the greatest reluctance – to his father.

The father took a long time to die and for that uncurtailable interval G was free from her husband's control. The power of death impressed and relieved her. She went to the country house with her daughter and her daughter's nanny, and spent her days in the virgin light and liberty of death. She did not go to her studio. The three of them sat together on a bench in the garden, talking. The nanny was a good talker. She told stories about her upbringing and her family, of which she was the ninth and last child. The sagas of the other eight, observed from this vantage point at the bottom, constituted the riveting plotlines of these stories. There were also stories of the nanny's life in service, which were sufficiently indiscreet to be very amusing. G heard herself laughing, there on the bench in the garden. The nanny had grown up in a small poor town where a main road passed right next to the houses. People were always being injured and sometimes even killed just outside their own front doors, the nanny said, and once an enormous truck actually drove through a house that stood on a bend of the road while the people were sleeping inside. G nearly laughed at that too, the image of the people sleeping up in the air in their little beds while beneath them was suddenly empty space. One time, the nanny said darkly, a woman was walking with her baby in a pram and when she tried to cross the road the truck didn't stop. It hit the pram and the woman was left standing empty-handed by the side of the road.

G's daughter was evidently familiar with these tales because her eyes would light up in anticipation of certain parts, and she would occasionally prompt the nanny's memory. It gave G a strange sensation, to see her child full of another woman's stories, as she might have been full of another woman's milk. She wondered whether her husband knew that this heady milk was flowing in their daughter's veins. In the morning she went into the kitchen and made pancakes. She made them carefully and neatly, as though from memory, despite the fact that she had no real memories of that kind. Her daughter and the nanny ate them eagerly and without question. They sat there like birds with open beaks and she gave them more. It was natural, she saw, for her to do such things. This capacity was like a perfectly functioning limb that she had never used. When she went into her studio in the garden, it appeared to her as the abandoned scene of her preoccupations. She left the door open, as the door of a house stands open at a death. Shutting the studio door had always been accompanied by a feeling of relief, a sort of click, as of two magnetised parts finally being permitted to meet. This sense of being reunited with herself was the corollary of her fear that one of these parts – the part that lived in the studio – had been displaced or mislaid and couldn't be found. Now the door to the studio remained open and G's daughter started to come in and out. G tidied up, or worked superficially on mostly finished canvases, not daring to concentrate. It occurred to G that there might exist a second G, a G who did not work. Her daughter sat on the studio couch, obliviously reading or drawing, with a natural air of entitlement. In a flash G saw how her working self, like a witch, could rise up and frighten the child or expel her. Who was this witch who saw her opportunity in the natural entitlement of children?

One afternoon G's daughter looked up from her book and asked G why there needed to be men. Why can't there just be mothers and children? she said. This bold and horrifying question immediately struck G as a trick. It was as though the walls were waiting for her answer. The answer seemed to be that there needed to be men because G thought men were superior. The idea of a world filled with mothers and children repelled her. It would be a world that lacked the crystalline force of judgement. If men were dispensable, then so was her desire for superiority. She identified mothers and children with mediocrity. How could that be, when she herself was a mother? Men are great, she answered. She justified this answer as encouraging a balanced attitude. But the question pierced her repeatedly in the days that followed. She saw how weak and compromised she was. She thought of her painter friend and knew that her daughter would have preferred a mother of that kind. The painter kept men casually in the shadows, and G saw that this was out of a deep and possibly impersonal distrust of them. The painter entirely lacked the desire for male freedom and prestige that was G's most visceral impulse.

G began to draw her daughter, childlike drawings that the girl herself could easily have bettered. She didn't look at her daughter while she drew: the drawings came from her hand. The hand was full of clumsiness and simplicity but it seemed to awaken to the sense of its task. Because G didn't look at her, the girl didn't know she was being observed. It was an interior act of pure attention. The observation was not an enquiry but a confirmation, like the chiming of a bell. She drew other things in this way, with a wavering unsteady line, her hand never leaving the paper. Unlike in her earlier drawings of childhood, she had no desire at all for obscenity. It was when she looked at the photographs of her daughter that hung everywhere in the house that she recognised obscenity. Her husband had a knack for eliciting a certain expression from the child, whose innocence was tainted in the same instant as it was recorded. This little act of violation was his pride, and he repeated it over and over. She saw that he mistook it for genius. One afternoon, her heart hammering in her chest, she took all the photographs down.

The nanny appeared satisfied with the direction G was taking, much as her old gallerist used to be when G embarked on a new phase of work. She deferred to G ceremoniously, a smile of contentment on her lips at every evidence of the proper order of things being restored. She too seemed to find it natural that the waters would flow forth from the dam that habitually held them in check. No one identified this ruptured dam as a catastrophe, but when G's husband returned it was immediately evident to them all that a disaster had occurred. He took in the scene of his displacement, the denuded walls, the atmosphere of female laxity, and straight away set to work rebuilding his authority. G heard his voice everywhere, loudly giving commands and administering judgement. The nanny coolly crossed back over to the other side and resumed her customary position as his subordinate. G felt the broken fences in herself, where her hatred had surged out and got free. Her husband saw that G had admitted to herself that she hated him. He was pale, almost bloodless, and though he spoke of his father's death as an unpleasantness he did not wish to discuss, she realised his strange pallor was that of fear. One afternoon she heard him calling for their daughter in the garden. The child was sitting on the studio couch while G sketched beside her in a chair. At the sound of his voice outside, their eyes met in silence. He called and called, with increasing anger. Finally they heard his footsteps come close and he appeared in the doorway of the studio. He was arrested for a moment by the sight of the child on the couch. His eyes moved to G in her chair, then with brisk fury he advanced across the room. G watched her daughter flinch as he approached. He took her by the arm and pulled her forcibly to her feet and led her squirming outside, shutting the door behind him.

In the spring we went back to Mann's farm. There was no one at home when we called at the farmhouse. The black dog, Lola, was roaming restlessly in the courtyard in front of the closed front door. She followed us up to the cottage, where Johann was working in the adjacent field. When he saw us he put down his spade and came to talk to us, stroking the dog's fine silky head. He told us that Mann's wife was in Germany but was expected back at any time. He said that her mother was dying.

The valley was greener and more radiant in springtime, and beside Johann's caravan the vegetables were sending out their shoots in neat rows. There were wildflowers all along the path to the sea and little songbirds sped joyously over the precipice and dived down toward the water. The abandoned house remained untouched but now there were horses there, grazing among the rocks in the clearing. Lola had begun to follow us on our walks. She ran madly back and forth across the hillside, leaping among the boulders, disappearing into bushes and then bursting out again. She startled the horses and sent the goats scrambling off in rivers of shale. Johann said that she had taken to roaming away from the farm, and he had even seen her up near the main road. The absence of Mann's wife unsettled her, he said. She knows that things are not as they should be.

Sometimes we saw Mann, in the farmyard or the fields around the house, but he seemed neither to see nor to remember us. He moved around as though entranced, his wild white head alert to something unseen. Often he would fold his elongated figure into a tiny, extraordinarily rusted car and speed away down the track and through the gates. He's going to meet his cronies in the town, Johann said, watching the vanishing car disgustedly. He told us to bring him the dog, the next time we wanted to go for a walk, and he would tie her up by his caravan.

One afternoon, as we were returning to the farm, we were overtaken by a dusty yellow bus that stopped outside Mann's gates. The doors opened and Mann's daughter stepped down onto the road. She was wearing a school uniform and carried a satchel on her shoulders. She greeted us politely and we followed her through the gates, where she turned not down the track toward the farmhouse but in the other direction, along a path that led in twists and turns up the hillside. One of the caravans that had once been in the olive grove now stood precariously up there, in a clearing facing the valley. There was a washing line with clothes neatly pegged to it and an awning over the door with a table and chairs beneath. The girl slowly picked her way up the path toward it, and as she approached the little dark figure of Grazia could be seen coming out from beneath the awning, her black scarf tied around her head.

In the evening Johann came to bring us some early vegetables from his garden, and he told us that Mann's wife had moved with her daughter and the housekeeper into the caravan.

She did it a few weeks ago, he said, as soon as the rains had stopped.

He sat on the upturned crate in which he had carried the vegetables, and opened a bottle of beer he had brought with him.

She should have got further away, he said, looking doubtfully up at the caravan, but there was nowhere else for her to go.

He described the ordeal of moving the caravan, which had to be dragged up the hill. They used the cattle to pull it up there, with the help of some young men from the village.

I thought we would all be killed, he said. One of the ropes broke and it nearly fell on top of us. I still don't know how we did it, he said. She got a huge strength from somewhere. I think it was her hatred.

Johann brought the bottle to his lips and tipped back

his head, so that the movement of his strong brown throat could be seen. Then his tanned, slightly lugubrious face reappeared with its long upper lip and fleshy nose and heavy-lidded pale eyes. He wiped his mouth with the back of his hand.

She hates him, he said ruefully, but it might have been easier just to push him over the ravine.

Things had been bad between them for a long time, he told us, but the crisis came when Mann's wife found out that Mann had been selling parcels of the farm behind her back. He's been doing it for years, Johann said. He would sell a portion of the land and then lease it back for his lifetime from the new owner. Not only that, Johann said, but he was so incompetent that he sold the portions for too little and agreed the leases at too high a price, so that very soon he was in need of more money than before he'd sold them and was forced to sell more. Everyone knew about it except her, Johann said, and she was bound to find out eventually, because he couldn't even be bothered to deceive her properly. But it wasn't the deception that disgusted her, he said. It was the idea that after all he only cared about the valley in the context of his own life. Despite everything, he said, she still saw him as the defender of this place, and now it turned out that it didn't matter to him what happened to it, as long as he wasn't there to see it. She could accept his selfishness on her own account, but what about their daughter?

The truth is, Johann said, that he doesn't care about the girl either. She's plain and she's decent and she doesn't gratify his vanity. He has women all over the island, he said, or at least he did before he started to look like a demented tramp. I've been married twice, Johann said, and divorced twice, and I've learned enough to know that these stories always have two sides, but in this case there's no other side. It's almost too clear, he said perplexedly. It's perhaps the only clear thing about Mann, he said, who otherwise makes a mess wherever he goes.

Two days later Mann's wife returned, and we met her one afternoon at the gates to the farm. A strong wind had sprung up on the island, which at night moaned and pressed around the eaves of the cottage, and we had thought of her and her daughter in the caravan, exposed on the clearing on the hill. She told us that she had gone back to Germany because her mother was about to die, and that it had not gone as she had expected. At first she had sat at her mother's bedside full of confusion, thinking about the absence of any love between them and wondering how they would go through this final chapter.

For a whole day and a night, she said, I sat beside her and listened to her terrible breathing. Sometimes she would open her eyes and look at me and I thought that she was finally going to say the words I have always

93

wanted to hear. I thought she was going to speak or make some sign, she said, but she just closed her eyes again, as if I was not the person she was hoping to see. On the morning of the second day, she said, there was a ring on the doorbell and I opened it and a young girl was standing there with a big backpack on her back. She was very small, with long black hair, and she said she had walked all the way from the station because she hadn't wanted to put us to the trouble of collecting her. I had no idea who she was, Mann's wife said, but she told me it had been arranged for her to come and look after my mother in her last hours. She would be with her every moment, she assured me, and would not leave her side, and if I could just show her where everything was in the apartment, I was free to leave.

Mann's wife stood facing into the wind, with her legs planted and her arms crossed, the expression of bewilderment on her face as she looked out through the gates toward the road.

So I showed her the apartment, she said, and then I went in to see my mother for the last time and I left. This morning the girl called me, she said, and told me that it was over. It had taken longer than she had expected because my mother had put up a very strong resistance. She said that she didn't know where my mother got her strength from, Mann's wife said, and I find I can't get that phrase out of my head, but I was glad it wasn't me who had to face her strength. I wonder about that girl, she said, who I suppose is going now with her backpack to another house. I never imagined that such a person existed.

She turned and looked up the hill toward the caravan, where her daughter stood in the doorway waiting for her. She waved, and the girl waved back. Mann's wife smiled.

The wind will stop tomorrow, she said. The weather is going to be nice.

It wasn't until the spring of the following year that we were able to return to Mann's farm. We stood and waited in the farmyard but the shutters were closed and the black dog Lola did not come out. From there the white crest of the mountain could be seen rearing mutely against the blue sky. It was impossible, we realised, to look at the mountain enough, for it would never become familiar nor have its strangeness mastered. It registered nothing: it forgot everything that it saw. It didn't remember that there had once been snow there.

There was no sign of Johann at the caravan in the clearing, and the vegetable garden was full of weeds. The caravan on the hill was still there, but its awning was broken and it was surrounded by piles of scrap metal and lumber. The cottage, however, had been prepared for us, with the key in the lock and a basket of provisions standing on the doorstep. It was just turning to dusk and a pale-pink light filled the sky. The great cacti silently held out their arms to receive the pink light. We put our bags inside and came back out, to look down the valley toward the sea.

The police came to G's house. They rang the doorbell, like travelling salesmen. They wanted to speak to her husband. Some photographs of G's daughter had been passed to them by the printer.

It was all a mistake, of course – it was just a silly confusion. G's husband was at his most inarguably charming and authoritative. G watched the policemen move from suspicion to receptiveness to acquiescence. They listened to his explanation, which was that he had been dissatisfied with the quality of some prints that came back from the printer, and had raised the issue with him. Call me old-fashioned, he said with winning self-deprecation, but I still use a film camera. I just can't get the hang of the digital ones, he said, and I actually think the quality of light might be better doing it the old way. The policemen were listening earnestly. The printer was a temperamental character, her husband continued, and he had obviously decided to get his own back, because as they could see these were simply normal family photographs. My wife is an artist, he said, putting his arm around G. So it's me who takes the family snaps. I obviously don't have her talent, he smiled.

After the policemen left, her husband, white with fear and anger, descended into a vicious rage that lasted for several days. He shouted at G and at their daughter. Once, G asked him a question while he was holding a coffee mug and he threw the mug at her. It hit her hard on her shoulder. You stupid woman, he said. Another time, when their daughter didn't want to wear her coat to school, he manhandled her into the coat so roughly that she cried. G began to think about running away from him. She thought about going and living somewhere on her own. The problem, as always, was her daughter's body. She wished, again, that they could share a body. Instead her body was shared between G and her husband. Her husband knew about her thoughts. He became quite calm and practical. He told her that she was free to leave, but that the house and the child would remain with him. He explained to her the reasons in law why this was so. He told her the amount of money she would be liable for. But if that's what you want, he said sadly, I won't stand in your way.

G went to her studio in the city. She stayed there all day without painting or moving. She sat in its disorder as the day grew dark outside the windows. She didn't turn on the lights.

The Diver

After the parade, a snow of litter and broken glass covered the streets which the municipal workers were already in the process of clearing up, blocking the main thoroughfares with their trucks so that it was impossible for the taxi to reach the restaurant.

We continued on foot, and though the driver had given us instructions it was difficult to find. The trucks moved slowly along the kerbs beside us in the hot dusk, pushing the garbage with their thick bristled skirts. In some places it lay a foot or more deep. It was mostly empty bottles and food packaging. People had eaten and drunk and thrown their packaging to the ground, as animals in the wild leave the carcass of what they have eaten on the ground. The windows of the storefronts showed the pink light from the sky.

We came to a narrow passageway that led into a concrete forecourt, where three men were loading sacks onto wooden pallets. When they saw us they pointed to another passageway on the opposite side and went back to what they were doing. The second passageway was darker and dirtier than the first. It turned left and right and then emerged into a further courtyard, this one adorned with globe-like lights and ornamental trees in giant pots and tables with white linen. It had vaulted sides, and the vaults had been fitted with glass, which reflected the tables and trees and made them seem more numerous. We saw Mauro and Julia sitting at a large table in the middle. Most of the other tables were still empty, and the replication of their image in the glass made it look as though the two of them were sitting in a field of vacant plots. We had been introduced to them earlier that day, before the incident at the museum had separated us. They had told us that they had grown up in the same small town in Italy without ever meeting, and had only met once they were living here in the city. Mauro was a professor and Julia was a curator at the museum, and together they had coordinated the conference about G.

Mauro sprang to his feet as we approached and congratulated us on finding the restaurant.

I'm afraid the others might not solve the riddle so quickly, he said. It's typical of this city's attitude to fashion, he said, that the most desirable meeting place should also be impossible to find.

Not so impossible, Julia observed, since they found it. It's the parade that has confused everything.

Mauro pulled out two chairs on the opposite side of the table.

In addition you may have noticed, he said, that they have chosen the most squalid location for their restaurant, as though we might be fooled into mistaking this latest temple of capitalism for something more authentic. Of course the bill will dispel that illusion quite thoroughly, but by then it will be too late.

Oh Mauro, said Julia, who had been eyeing him cynically during this speech, can't we just be quiet for once and relax? Personally I like it here, she said, they've made it feel like a little Italian piazza, and the weather is so nice. We don't need to find fault with everything, especially since the museum will be paying the bill.

Before Mauro could reply, his phone rang and he jumped up from the table again to answer it.

I used to admire Mauro for criticising everything, Julia said while he paced around the pale gravel in the falling dusk. I thought it meant he was intelligent. Then I realised that while he was outraged everyone else was just having a good time. Thankfully he isn't my husband, she said, so I am able to love him anyway.

Julia was a handsome woman with flowing dark hair and a beret set at a piratical angle on her head. She had a wide, flat face which she held very still and balanced, like a serpent, her mouth wearing a laconic smile and her slanting green eyes unblinking.

That was the director, Mauro announced when he returned. The police have finally let her go, so she's on her way here.

At last, Julia said. They kept her so long I was worried they'd found something to accuse her of.

Obviously there was a lot of paperwork to fill in for the police, Mauro explained to us, as well as for the museum's own protocol. And then of course all the people who witnessed the incident had to be examined as to their mental state and the protocol re-examined in the light of it and more paperwork filled in, he said, when in fact there is nothing to do, nothing that can be done in a situation as evidently irreversible as this one. And since no one knew the man, no one can actually claim to have been harmed by what he did. Meanwhile, he concluded, we continue our existences in great comfort here in this charming spot.

Why don't you order some wine? Julia said to him. It will make your audience more appreciative.

Mauro picked up the wine list from the table and bent his fierce, neat face over it. His small head and tightly curled black hair gave him a ram-like appearance. He wore enormous white-framed glasses which he removed to read the wine list.

Despite what Julia says, he resumed, I reserve the

right to analyse what is put in front of my eyes, especially when it comes to things that have apparently been created for my pleasure. It's true that I wish not to be taken for a fool, he said, but also I find something deathly in the interference of illusion with reality.

Through the vaulted windows he summoned a waiter, who shortly came out to our table. He took Mauro's order impassively and went quickly away again.

He did not approve of my choice, Mauro said with a shrug. First I did not ask for his advice, and then he saw that I simply chose the second-cheapest bottle on the list, which is what I always do. To be made to feel you are in Italy, he continued, addressing Julia, when you are not in fact in Italy seems to me the saddest thing in the world. It is sad in the way dreams are, because they reveal something fundamentally confused in our grasp of truth. Nothing is more pitiful than to watch a dog dreaming he is chasing a rabbit, partly because a dog is one of the few creatures we can observe in this way, knowing what he thinks he is doing while seeing that he is not in fact doing it. I refuse to be that dog, he said, thinking that I am in Italy while the owner of this restaurant watches me through a spy-hole and rubs his hands together.

There's Betsy, Julia said, standing up and waving at a couple who had just entered the courtyard. Mauro sprang up again to pull out a chair for the woman, who seemed to have difficulty walking and who collapsed into it with a great groan, extending one leg stiffly out to the side.

Thank you, Mauro, she panted, closing her eyes and letting her head loll back over the chair. I couldn't believe it when the driver said we had to get out and walk. I'm sure that's illegal. Thank God I had David with me.

David had taken a seat at the far end of the table and was looking at his phone. Betsy gave another groan and then straightened up a little in her chair.

I said, can't you see I'm a cripple? Just because people have thrown garbage all over the streets to celebrate their freedom, that means cripples have to walk? Bless you, she said to Julia, who had offered her a glass of water. What sort of anarchy is this supposed to be, she said, where the city rushes straight in to clean up the results of its own tolerance? It's like some browbeaten mother sneaking in to clean up her teenager's bedroom. They should have made them clean it up themselves. Not to mention the thousands of police being paid overtime and the doctors and ambulances on standby – if I lived here, she said, I wouldn't be too happy about paying my taxes.

The waiter was filling people's glasses with wine and David drank the contents of his in one swallow and pushed it back across the table to be refilled.

We should recognise the consequences of freedom for what they are, he said, in a gruff monotone.

Oh nonsense, Betsy said to him. I call that depressive. When did freedom become synonymous with lack of self-control?

You never told us you hurt your leg, Julia said reproachfully. We would have made different arrangements if we'd known.

I tripped on the pavement and twisted it, Betsy said. Where I live, they compensate you when that happens, as if it's the pavement's fault. In this case the pavement had buckled because of the roots of a tree that had grown under it. So then it was the tree's fault. Now they're going to cut it down. It's a big beautiful oak tree that grows right opposite my house. I look at it every day. I don't want them to cut it down. But the tree hurt you, they say. I say, if I refuse the compensation and deny I was hurt, will you stop cutting down the tree?

I suppose someone else might be hurt the same way, said Julia.

That's just what they say, said Betsy. I say, if that happens then let her be the one to make the decision.

But it looks quite serious, said Mauro. You can barely walk.

That's because I'm too fat, said Betsy, and I didn't do the exercises they gave me at the hospital.

David gave a snort of laughter.

Why didn't you do them? said Mauro, bemused.

I didn't want to, said Betsy.

She was a short, round woman in late middle age with an abundance of springy grey hair and an expression of mild surprise in her round blue eyes. She was swathed in a colourful wrapper and wore a great quantity of rattling jewellery.

My ambition all my life, she said to Mauro, has been to avoid the things people say you have to do. I made the discovery quite early that you could avoid them, and now there's no way I can make myself do them if I don't want to. There are some positive aspects to living that way, but when the dictators take over I suppose I'll be the first one to be shot.

Yet you require others to have self-control, Mauro observed, and to clean up after their own parade.

You're right, Betsy said cheerfully. It's an individual position. It's probably my mother's fault – if I didn't want to go to school she would say fine, don't go. One time I had a big part in a school play and I was so nervous she called them before the performance and said I was sick. I still remember that evening, she said, sitting at home knowing the play was going on without me. I kept looking at my watch to see which line I would have been saying at that moment. It seemed incredible to me not to be there, having learned my part and gone to all the rehearsals. I felt like I had discovered a whole new world that no one else knew about.

But that's terrible! Mauro exclaimed. Was she the same if you didn't want to go to the dentist, or didn't want to put on your seatbelt in the car?

I always wanted to go to the dentist, Betsy said slightly haughtily. He was a lovely man.

She accepted a glass of wine from the waiter and sat back in her chair.

I shouldn't have said it was my mother's fault, she resumed presently. People are always blaming their mothers for things. I expect she thought she was teaching me that I could have power, and most people don't teach little girls that. But the fact remains, she said, that because I don't do the exercises my leg doesn't get better.

Here's the director at last, Mauro said, waving his hand at the woman who had just entered the courtyard. When she saw him she gave a weary grimace.

She looks so tired, Julia said.

She has a right to be, Betsy said. There should be a strategy to deal with people who decide to kill themselves in public places. At home I take a commuter train to work and back again every day, and at least twice a week someone decides to throw themselves on the line. You see the havoc it wreaks, everyone suddenly on their phones having to change their plans, stressed-out women trying to get back from the office to their children, people missing their connections, people who are exhausted or disabled and just need to get home, and you wonder why more isn't being done. I had the idea that they should just put a booth by the tracks where you could go in and do the job without bothering everyone. They could even put a simulator in there, she said matter-of-factly, with the sound of the train coming.

David gave another snort of laughter and slowly shook his head.

The director arrived at the table and stood looking at us wanly.

I'm so sorry, she said. I don't know what to say.

Mauro found a chair for her and she sat down and rummaged in her handbag for a tissue, with which she noisily blew her nose. Her face, which was extraordinarily narrow and bony, was red. Her small pink-rimmed eyes were so pale that they were almost colourless. They carried an expression of great strain that seemed to extend beyond the day's events. Presently she collected herself and addressed the table in a high, trembling voice.

In the taxi here, she said, I was trying to think of how I could possibly sum up or explain what happened today, when each person's journey toward these events was so different. For me it had obviously involved months of planning and preparation, she said, in which I tried to foresee everything that could possibly go wrong, without of course even considering they might go wrong in the way they did. The violence of what happened, she said, which in an instant destroyed all these arrangements, seemed both pointless in itself, and also to give an impression of our work and our values as pointless, that they could so easily be swept away. It was this feeling of fragility, almost of absurdity, that I was thinking about in the taxi. It might seem rather ridiculous, she said, and even irrelevant, to spend your time curating artistic events and organising talks and discussions about artists, when the slightest change in reality can render those activities obsolete or impossible. But then it struck me, she said, that what happened at the museum today reminded me of nothing so much as a work by G herself. The power of disturbance in G's work, she said, seems linked to the actual disturbances of reality such as the one we witnessed, but I haven't yet been able to formulate any thoughts about that link.

She stared down at her hands, which were clenched around the tissue.

As well as being a catastrophe in obvious ways, she resumed, it was also personally a great pity for me, because this was to be my last public event as director.

I will shortly be stepping down from my role, she said, though the exhibition will of course remain in place for its full run and will then travel around the world. I believe it will have a lasting impact in terms of the public perception of G's persona and of the significance of her art. G found a radical honesty in her last years, she said, which sheds a new light on everything she had done before. I hope I will be able to hear at least some of your thoughts on that subject over the course of this evening, she said, even if the audience sadly can't.

There was a smattering of applause around the table. The noise of garbage trucks could still be heard from beyond the high walls. People were coming into the courtyard and the waiters in their black uniforms were emerging from behind the glass vaults. A large group of people in wigs and masks and elaborate costumes arrived, evidently on their way from the parade.

You haven't told me what it actually is you're going to do next, Mauro said to the director. Is it a secret? It must be something very important, since you're leaving when the show has only just opened and since I can't think of a more prestigious job than the one you already have.

In fact, the director said, I don't have another job.

But what are you going to do? asked Julia.

I'm not going to do anything, the director said. She searched in her bag for another tissue and blew her nose again. Excuse me, she said, it's been a rather difficult day.

Of course, Julia said, putting a hand on the director's arm. You've had quite a shock.

I grew up on a farm, the director said. I'm perfectly used to the sight of death. No, it was all the bureaucracy that was maddening. And of course other people's reactions, though a lot of the staff are quite young, so I suppose you have to forgive them. But nobody knew this man – what did it matter to them? I just wish he had chosen another day, she said drily. To answer your question, she said to Mauro, I'm leaving because I'm moving away. I'm moving to one of the islands, where there are no museums, and where I've been lucky even to find a school for my daughter. It is a little school with only one class that has all the island's children in it. I will take her there every morning and I will come back to collect her every afternoon, and if she likes she can even come home for lunch.

I see, Mauro said, smiling and showing his rather small and pointed teeth. You are taking a philosophical position. I hope the people on this island live up to their part of the bargain.

Perhaps you don't approve, the director said, and you're not the only one, but in the end what difference does it make? Someone else will be made director of the museum and will do a perfectly good job of it. People have asked me whether I won't be sad to leave the world of museums and public art, especially in the light of this exhibition, which was really a victory for us and is the most significant thing we've done, but I'm not particularly sad. I was walking around it today, she said, as if I were an ordinary person, just looking, and it struck me how strange it is, how actually bizarre, that some people take it into their heads to create objects for the rest of us to look at. Psychologists tell us that little children are proud of their own shit, and enjoy showing it to other people, until they are informed that their shit is disgusting and should be hidden, and I suddenly wondered whether artists somehow never got this message and kept on being proud of their shit and wanting to show it to people.

Mauro gave a bark of laughter. But isn't that precisely the way they help us? he said. Isn't that why we go and look at their shit, as you call it? Because we have been made ashamed of our own?

The director sat back in her chair and folded her arms across her lap.

At certain times of day, she said presently, when the museum isn't full, the atmosphere is like that of a church. You can tell people are attributing sanctity to these works of art, and some godlike capacity to the artists who created them. At other times the museum is crowded and the atmosphere completely changes. People push and shove each other trying to see, like people trying to see the aftermath of a car crash or some equally gruesome spectacle. They take photos with their phones, like voyeurs, and in fact sometimes I think they don't even see what it is they're photographing. They're just making a copy to take away with them, and somewhere in that process they turn what is meant to be eternal into something disposable. It's hard not to feel, she said, that the works are damaged or diminished in some way by all these millions of copies that are taken from them.

Why don't you ban photography? Mauro said. It's what some museums do.

I did ban it, the director said. I put up signs, and told the curators to enforce the rule, but people ignored the signs and the curators were driven mad by having to police the situation. They became accusatory and dictatorial, and this behaviour was the worst thing of all because it created an atmosphere of petty tyranny in the museum that made the artworks seem fragile and sanctimonious. So we took the signs down because in the end people can do what they want, she said. It isn't up to me to stop them.

The air was still thick with heat but the blue of evening had started to collect in the courtyard. The shapes of people and objects began to grow harder and more distinct, as though with the departure of light they were acquiring substance. The restaurant was becoming crowded. Suddenly the globe-like lamps were switched on, and the golden floating shapes swam mysteriously over the darkening mass of heads.

You know, the director said, I was actually walking around the show at the same time as the man.

Did you notice him? said Mauro.

I admit I did, the director said. He was acting strangely, by which I mean that there was something unusual about him that I couldn't identify. I followed him through the rooms for a while out of suspicion. He was drifting around the place in a sort of trance. Then he started walking in circles, circling the works one after another, and it reminded me of the way an animal circles before it lies down to sleep. I thought he might be drunk or on drugs. He was very slender, and perhaps that's what reassured me and made me feel that he wasn't likely to cause any damage, even if that doesn't seem to make much sense. But the works are very large and strong and he seemed small and weak by comparison. At that moment my phone rang, she said, and I had to step outside onto the walkway to answer it. As you know, she said, in that upper gallery each room has access out to the walkway that looks all the way down the atrium to the bottom floor. It is right under the glass roof, so the light there is extraordinary. I was proud of our decision to set up the exhibition in that space, she said, even though it is less convenient than some of the lower galleries. It seemed the ideal environment for G's work, that loftiness and light, the feeling one has up there of being somehow suspended in space. Some of G's pieces, she said, also utilise this quality of suspension in achieving disembodiment, which for me at times seems the furthest one can go in representing the body itself.

It was actually my ex-husband on the phone, she said, who is very angry about my decision to move to the island with our daughter, and who is calling me at the moment several times a day. Each time he calls, it is to deliver a shot of poison to me. I didn't want to go all the way downstairs to take my shot of poison, so I just stayed where I was on the walkway at the top of the atrium. I was standing right there beside the railings, on my phone, when the man came out and threw himself over. The strange thing is, she said, that I watched it happen without saying anything about it to my ex-husband. He had no idea that, while we were talking, a man had come out of the gallery and thrown himself over the railings a metre from where I stood. He was saying the most horrible things to me, she said, things that only he knows how to say and yet that seem at the same time to be generated from inside myself. I was listening to this hate-filled voice when my eyes saw the man move past me and launch himself into empty space. It seemed to me that the whole thing happened in silence, she said, perhaps because my ex-husband was talking while it was going on. This impression I had, she said, that the man hadn't made a sound, seemed to turn his actions into something for which my ex-husband was responsible. It was as if the man were being directed to destroy himself, as my ex-husband would like me to destroy myself. He was dressed entirely in black, she said, including a black cap on his head, and these sombre clothes added to my sense that I was looking at some kind of projection, some embodiment of the will of my ex-husband, who, as I have said, wishes I would throw myself over those railings in much the same way. It would of course have been difficult for anyone to make sense straight away of so shocking and unexpected a sight, she said, but what was surprising was how natural I found it, this explanation that my ex-husband's arrogance and hatred had got out into the world and were driving people to destroy themselves.

There was a sudden roar of laughter from one of the neighbouring tables and the director gave a start, her eyes darting around the courtyard.

After that, she continued presently, there were a few seconds of silence while the man was falling, and I knew that pandemonium would erupt at any moment. Those seconds seemed to last an eternity, and in that time I realised that by watching the man jump over the railings without conveying this fact to my ex-husband, I had demonstrated an extraordinary separation from him. It was a separation more complete than I would have thought it was possible to have from another human being. I realised that it was possible to have power over him, something that has never even occurred to me in all the time I have known him. In a way it was the man who gave me that gift of realisation, and perhaps it is only my upbringing that allows me to see death itself as a gift. I was taught not to mourn when things die. I was taught that when things die they give strength and substance back to the world. They enable our survival, as well as giving space for what is new. For the same reason I have always believed that my ex-husband will never die, she said, because he lacks the basic generosity to do so.

The waiters were walking around the table filling the glasses with wine. The director leaned back in her chair so that they could reach across her, her pale, rinsed eyes staring out across the restaurant. Darkness had fallen and most of the tables were full. Around us now was a noisy ferment of faces and voices and the crashing sounds of glasses and cutlery. Many people had come from the parade and their fantastical costumes gave something phantasmagoric and dreamlike to the scene. Through

116

the glass vaults the lit-up kitchen was now visible, a panorama of smoke and fire where men and women in aprons and caps worked industriously, their faces shining with sweat. Mauro suggested that we shortly order some food before the kitchen became overwhelmed.

Don't make me panic, Betsy said. I refuse to compete for resources with people in police outfits and Barbie wigs.

She picked up her menu and gave her instructions, which were lengthy, to the waiter.

I like to think I don't shock easily, she said to the director while the others gave their orders, but I have to admit you've taken me by surprise, and not only because of your unsentimental attitude to what happened. What feels shocking is the way things happen to you that don't seem to happen to anyone else. This husband of yours, for instance, who calls you up all the time wishing you were dead, not to mention the idea that you have to leave your job to go and hide with your child on an island. The violence of what happens to you, she said to the director, seems connected in some way that I can't understand with your lack of self-pity, but also with your success. I myself don't see life as violent, she said, and maybe the result is that certain things don't happen to me. You say you had a brutalising childhood, she said, but how did this violence get so tangled up with your responsibilities and achievements? It's almost as though you think that's what a woman has to put up with if she wants to distinguish herself.

The director was watching her expressionlessly while she spoke. Betsy's colourful garments and jewellery contrasted with the severity of the director's narrow tailored suit.

It's a terrible thought, the director replied presently, that we cause our own reality. I'm not sure I believe it's true. I don't hold myself responsible for other people's violence, though it's probably the case that my ambition has exposed me to more dramatic events than is usual. But it may also be that I suffer less than other people in the end, she said, because I've learned to see things on a larger scale. The worst sufferings I have seen have always been those that are most intimate and personal. I have a friend, for instance, who is in a relationship with a man who has a child. My friend doesn't have children, she said, and so she didn't realise that for this man the child will always be more important than she is. The torture she goes through, the director said, a thousand times every day when the man reveals this fact by some minor word or action is quite extraordinary. She knows that it is wrong to be jealous of a child, yet this knowledge seems to propel her deeper into the situation, so that the child must be to blame and has become actually abhorrent to her. She talks about it to anyone who will listen, like an addict, and like an addict she doesn't seem to realise how much she exposes her own weakness to the judgement of other people. When I think about her life in their small apartment, the director said, where a thousand times each day she feels knives of jealousy and rejection plunge into her flesh, I feel quite relieved to experience the tangible, open violence of my own life, where at least everyone can see and understand what's going on.

I'm backing your friend, said Betsy. I can't stand all this sanctity around parenthood. Why should a grown woman be relegated to the back seat by the existence of a child? What's wrong with this man, that he treats the product of his own loins as front-page news? She should give her love to someone who knows how to value it. You just need to look at the artists who had children, she said, to find some of the worst instances of neglect in the annals of parenthood. Obviously I'm not advertising that as a strategy, she said. My point is that this is what a true passion looks like. G herself, Betsy added, was not without sin when it came to motherhood.

She picked up her wine glass and sipped neatly from it, her eyes travelling mildly around the courtyard.

I admit I sometimes wonder, Mauro said, why so many artists have children if it's only to treat them badly. I would have expected that they of all people would know how serious a business it is to bring something into the world. In the case of the men, I suppose it's at least possible that it was their wives that wanted a child and not them. But for the women, he said, the decision – when it is a decision and not an unplanned event – to invite something into your life that will directly and intimately sabotage your capacity to work is slightly mystifying. My mother wanted to be a writer, he said, and she always blamed us, her children, for the fact that she never succeeded. Yet what I remember is that she would go into her room and lock the door and for many hours at a time we were forbidden to disturb her. Over and over again, he said, as a small child, I would feel the impulse to see my mother and I would run to find her, only to remember that she was behind the locked door. I would stand in the corridor outside that door, feeling the strongest desire to bang on it and alert her to my presence, while knowing how angry she would be with me if I did. Of course the memory of the door, and of how I felt standing on the wrong side of it, has remained with me, he said, but over time its meaning has changed. The door was in fact the door to my mother, and she locked it in the hope of giving expression to herself, but the expression didn't come. It was as if she went in there to look for something and was unable to find it. When she was old, he said, I very gently reminded her of that time, in the hope of receiving an explanation, and she claimed not to remember anything about it. The mystery was so complete, he said, that it couldn't even be spoken of. Recently, he said, I was reading about a woman artist, a sculptor, who makes all her work with her children. She has four or five children, he said, and she invites them into her studio, and they sit on the floor and play, or make things of their own, or sometimes even help her with what she is doing. This image, he said, which I have to admit brought tears to my eyes, and which is perhaps just that, an image, and not the whole truth, made me think about the struggles of my mother. By trying to separate herself from us, when it was too late because we already existed, perhaps she destroyed her own capacity to create. I have always felt great guilt toward artists, he said, and especially female artists, which I suppose is one reason why I try to understand and promote them. You might say I found my ideal subject in G, who used her experience of motherhood in a way that seemed to explain the subject to me much more clearly. What her work helps me to understand is that the impulse to have a child is very often a response to the woman's own childhood, as though her childhood has left her incomplete, or has taken a part of her that she is driven to find again. The struggle, he said, which is sometimes a direct combat, between the search for completeness and the desire to create art therefore becomes a core part of the artist's development. Because G didn't lock her door on her children, he said, it was much harder for her to succeed than for a male artist to succeed, but in the end the possibilities of her art became much larger.

But Mauro, Julia said, doesn't everybody feel their mother could have been an artist? Maybe we feel that way because we are guilty of wrecking our mothers' lives. Everybody wonders what their mothers were like before, or what they would have been if they hadn't had us. Or maybe it's just that we are egotistical and like to see ourselves as artworks, she said, and so we want to give prestige to the person who created us. As far as I can see, she said, the problems start only when the mother already is a genuine artist.

Julia removed her beret and her appearance became all at once less cavalier and more sober. She pushed her dark hair behind her shoulders.

Personally I take the question of G's childhood differently, she said. Her childhood was very conventional, and she herself carried the vestiges of conventionality into the early part of her life, which is what drove her to get married to a bourgeois man and become a mother. She made a conventional prison for herself, Julia said, which it took her many years to break out of. It's true that she didn't actually neglect her children, but the specific violence of her work toward the subject of motherhood and the female body must have been quite disturbing for them. The truth is, she said, that most people have children out of convention. It's only afterward that they start attaching all their ideas about creativity to them, because for most people a child is the only thing they've ever actually produced. My own mother treated me as though I was something very fragile and precious, she said, and the only dramas were about whether I was wearing a warm enough coat for the weather that day. I also used to wonder what she would have become, if she hadn't given all her time and attention to me. But as I got older I began to realise that she saw me not as myself but as something she had created, something that was important only because it belonged to her. Once, she said, I was at my daughter's school play, and I happened to be sitting behind a mother who was film-ing the whole thing on her phone. I kept looking at the screen, which was moving around in a distracting way, and after a while I realised that this woman was filming only her own daughter as she moved around the stage, leaving out the rest of the cast and turning the play into something nonsensical. It summed something up for me, Julia said, about my own childhood, where the importance I assumed began to change the structure of reality itself.

Hallelujah, Betsy said as the waiters approached across the gravel bearing trays of food. My blood sugar was starting to affect my focus, she said. Even the most thrilling onversation, she said, accepting her plate, can't hold me when I'm hungry.

What are G's children like? Julia said to David, who had been staring absently around him while the others talked, mechanically draining and refilling his wine glass from a bottle that stood in front of him on the table. He looked up, vaguely startled.

They're pretty old, said David. I wouldn't necessarily describe them as children. They're old guys with wrinkles and bellies.

You must know them quite well, Julia said.

That's right, David said.

Did you see much of their relationship with her? Julia said.

David shrugged. Some, he said. Like I said, they're old guys.

He frowned and wrinkled his brow.

I think she stopped being their mother a long time ago, he added after a while. She became a different person. The person who had those children was in the past, or maybe she was in the future. I always had the feeling, he said, that G was getting younger instead of older.

I don't think I know the story of how you became

involved with her, Mauro said. I seem to remember you were quite young.

David made a face, as though at the taste of something bad in his mouth.

I was twenty-five, he said. It isn't much of a story. My friend was working for her, helping out in her studio. He had to leave, and he asked if I wanted the job instead.

Mauro smiled. And somehow thirty years later you are responsible for the entire management of her legacy, he said.

I just stuck around, David said grimly. There was never anything else I particularly wanted to do. I didn't want to study.

She adored him, Betsy interposed. She adored young men generally, but especially him. He replaced the sons with the wrinkles and the bellies. If it wasn't for David, she said, I would never have got my smallest toe over the threshold of that place. I certainly wouldn't have been able to write the biography, not in a million years. When it came to young women, Betsy said, G was not quite so enthusiastic. The first time I interviewed her I was in my late twenties, and not terribly self-assured, and I asked her a question that she took exception to, she said, looking at David. I can't even remember what it was.

It was about scale, David said. It was about the legitimacy for a female artist of producing large-scale works.

Oh that's right, said Betsy. She thought I was accusing her of some kind of gratuitous machismo in making these big figures, and I admit on reflection that I probably didn't express myself in the most tactful way. But all the same, I wasn't expecting the reaction I got. She completely froze, and her face took on the most terrible expression, an expression almost of hatred – I was terrified, Betsy said, I thought she was about to brain me with her chisel. And then she gets up, and she picks up her chair, and she turns it around so that she has her back to me! For the rest of the interview she would only speak to me indirectly, through David. I would ask a question and she would say to David, '*She* wants to know the origin of my relationship to fabrics', in a tone of the utmost ridicule. It was the most humiliating experience of my life, Betsy said.

But didn't it make you hate her? Julia said. How could you go on to write the biography, and the essays, and to come to museums like ours to give talks about her?

Oh, I didn't take it personally, Betsy said. I don't tend to feel shame all that often – probably I should feel it more. But it isn't easy to make me ashamed, which was what G wanted and tried to do. I feel sorry for people who rely on shame, she said. It just shows that they were humiliated and shamed themselves, which was certainly the case with G. Her whole upbringing rested on shame as the central pillar, Betsy said. But my mother taught me not to be ashamed of myself and not to respond to bullying by criticising myself. Though I admit I did kick myself for making an enemy of her so early on in the process. It made things awfully difficult at times.

She never warmed to you, David observed.

She did not, Betsy said. But it didn't matter. I would never expect a woman like that to warm to a woman like me in any case. I'm fat and lazy and I like my comforts, and I've never risked anything in my life. I moved to the town where I live because it doesn't challenge me and because I can do what I want there. I chose to have friends instead of a family because it was less work. I chose a job in a mediocre college where they pay me a big stipend to write about the things that interest me. I'm happy, and I only ever wanted to be happy, and for a woman like G happiness is not only not a goal, it's an actual danger. I don't deny that she achieved happiness in her work, Betsy said, but I imagine it was happiness of so exalted a kind that most people would be incapable of understanding it. The ordinary forms of happiness were beneath her.

I think you're being overly modest, Mauro said. Your biography of G is an exceptional piece of interpretation. Your essays have changed the way people think about her, and have made her work accessible to a much wider public.

Well, if that's so, she never thanked me for it, Betsy said. I've had plenty of gratitude from artists I've done far less for. But I respect G for being ungrateful. She refused to be grateful. She refused to see herself as the victim of any of the things that happened to her. To tell you the truth, Betsy said, some of the women I've stuck up for disappoint me by being so grateful, and in the end you can see it in their work. G was selfish and cruel and egotistical – she was as bad as any man, and she was as good as any man. Better, in my opinion, because she lived two lives. First she lived the life of a woman, all crushed and conventional, making art on the side in between serving dinner to her husband's work col- leagues. Then, when he had the good manners to die and leave her financially comfortable, she lived the life of a man. What I don't know, Betsy said, is what would have happened if he'd stuck around, and to that extent a woman artist is always a victim of chance. She might be lucky and find that people give her some freedom, or she might stay crushed by the decisions that were forced on her along the way. At least G had the sense not to marry another artist, she said, though in fact that was a product of her conventionality too. She married a respectable, well-connected man, as she had been brought up to do. Where women have gone wrong, she said, is in mistaking an unconventional man as their chance for freedom. The worst stories of female sabotage in the arts are always those ones. A woman artist marries a male artist because she sees her ambitions mirrored in him. She thinks that because he's an artist he'll let her be an artist – she thinks he's the one guy who will understand her. But a male artist wants a slave, and when he marries a woman artist he gets the bonus of a slave who thinks he's a genius.

She said she had never been in love, David said. She despised love. It was one of the reasons she was so easy to be around.

Only if you were male, Betsy said. The woman who refuses to love can't tolerate other women. She knows they'll look down on her or pity her. And besides, she thinks they're idiots.

It's a terrible notion, Julia said, that a woman can be an artist only if she refuses to love.

If you ask me, David said, any woman is better off without love.

The dark hot night had deepened, and in the courtyard a state of fever seemed briefly to mount as the sounds of conversation and laughter converged and became indistinguishable, and the waiters hurried among the packed tables with loaded trays. A man was approaching our table through the crowd, and when the director noticed him she stood up. He was enormously tall and bony, with a large bald head and round, unblinking eyes and a somewhat ghoulish appearance. Despite the heat of the evening he wore a stiff dark coat.

Thomas, she said, what a pleasure – I had no idea you were here.

They put me in the corner behind a potted plant, the man said, like an ugly piece of furniture. I could see you but you couldn't see me.

This doesn't seem like the kind of place you would usually frequent, said the director, smiling.

I never have, Thomas said. But this evening I was walking past and I decided to come in.

He stared while the others found a chair and made space for him around the table.

If you're sure I won't be interrupting you, he said. I tried to go to the exhibition this afternoon, he said to the director, but the museum was closed. They said there had been an emergency of some kind. I was worried about you.

There was an accident, the director said. The whole building had to be evacuated. We had a day of lectures and talks programmed and it all had to be cancelled. Some of the people at this table came from halfway across the world to speak, she said, so it's been a great disappointment.

How unfortunate, Thomas said, his eyes bulging as he looked around the table. And presumably now you all have to go back across the world again. It must feel strange, as if you came here to create silence. I saw an ambulance outside the museum, he said to the director. I hope it wasn't anything too serious.

Serious enough, the director said. A man killed himself inside the museum space. He jumped from the top floor down into the atrium.

He made sure he saw the exhibition first, said Mauro. There's a sort of politeness in that.

Mauro, said Julia, that's a terrible thing to say.

There weren't many visitors there at the time, the director said, so it could easily have been worse. Because of the parade we didn't have the usual weekend crowds. But you can imagine all the protocol that we've had to face, and I'm sure that's far from over.

It seems inconsiderate, said Thomas, to do something so private in a public place. But perhaps he just didn't want to die alone. I wonder why he chose that exhibition to make his statement? Do you know?

I admit I've wondered about it, the director said. Of course he could have chosen it at random and there might be no connection at all. But it's true that he walked around the gallery first. I'm not saying that the works played any role in what he did, she said, since he surely must have decided to do it in advance. But I wonder whether they contributed something, the way dreams do. I wonder whether they loosened his association with reality. G's work, and particularly the work in this exhibition, does present a challenge to reality. It is the reality of the body that it questions. One treats the body as something concrete and immutable, she said, as something more real in a sense than the mind, yet separated from it, with no mind of its own. It is this hidden or unknown mind of the body, she said, where the body becomes more psychological and less real, that G was able to penetrate. I myself, she said, find something genuinely disturbing in the work, something for which I am able to find no explanations or answers, as though one's conscious response to it is somehow irrelevant, and it is the body – or the body's mind – that is responding. When I look at her work I feel how bizarre it is, how actually horrifying, to be located in a body, not because the body ages and dies, but because it is unknown to us. The people who try to know their bodies, through sport for instance, or pleasure, seem to me as limited and confined as people who practise religion. G's knowledge is entirely different, she said, her work is a spectacle both of horror and of freedom, and so I wonder whether the man at least felt that his actions would be understood in that environment.

You don't mention the physical pain involved in such an act, Thomas said when she had finished, nor what the body's mind makes of its pain. I wonder sometimes whether we have ceased in our age to take pain all that seriously. We have come to value psychological trauma more highly. Personally I have always been frightened of pain, he said. The first thing I thought, when you told me about the man jumping, was that I would be incapable of doing such a thing. I would be too frightened of the pain it would involve. Yet psychological pain doesn't frighten me at all. To the extent that I even feel it, I simply expect myself to bear it.

But Thomas, the director said, that is precisely how our particular past marked us. We feel things differently to other people.

Do you really think so? Thomas said. I think we probably experienced our own lives as completely normal – we didn't have anything to compare them to. It was only later that we discovered we had survived things that other people saw as traumatic. It doesn't feel that way to us – don't you agree? I don't feel any fear of emotional hurt and upset. Yet I don't see myself as brave. I see myself as a coward.

But surely those two things are connected, Mauro said to him. Isn't it the emotional numbness that creates the fear of physical sensation? When people feel things very strongly they usually stop worrying about what the consequence will be for their body. If you were defending your child, for instance, you might put yourself in harm's way without thinking about it.

I don't have a child, said Thomas, but I've thought often about that question. I know that it is treated almost as an accepted fact, that you would rush into a burning building to save your child, but what if it isn't true? The problem is that you will find very few people willing to testify for the other side. Who would admit that instead of rushing in, they acted instinctively to save themselves? Only once, he said, have I heard someone make such an admission, a young woman I knew who had just had a baby. She was very frightened of dogs, and when the baby was only a few weeks old she took her to the park. While she was holding the baby in her arms a big dog ran toward them, barking, and before she knew what she was doing she thrust the baby out in front of her as a kind of shield. It was completely instinctive, she said afterward, but she was horrified by her behaviour and thought it meant she was unfit to be a mother. Yet she was a very good mother, he said, and it was only this automatic reflex that had made her doubt it.

At least your friend had the excuse that the dog represented an actual danger, Julia said to Thomas, though I suppose that's precisely what makes her story shocking. But I know people who are incapacitated by the presence of birds or mice or even insects, and I've often wondered what it means. I suppose you would describe these as phobias, and maybe they are worse in people who live in cities and are estranged from the natural world, but if we are talking about courage it does seem an incredible vulnerability. One time, she said, a woman rang on my doorbell saying she was my neighbour, though I'd never seen her before. She was around my age, and very well dressed, and she explained that while she was out at work some pigeons had got into her apartment through a window she had left slightly open. She asked whether I could come and get rid of them for her, because she had a phobia of pigeons. I had to tell her that I also had a phobia of pigeons, Julia said, and that I could not go into her apartment. We stood there, two grown women who were complete strangers, in this ridiculous predicament. Eventually she sighed and went off down the street to ring another person's bell, and I realised it could easily have been me, unable to return to my own apartment because there was a pigeon there. In that moment it did seem very strange to me, she said in puzzlement, to have built a whole identity, with a personal and professional life, with friends and memories and problems of my own, that could completely collapse in the presence of a grey bird.

Mauro put his hand comfortingly on Julia's arm and she took his hand and held it.

I think it's because animals have no language, he said to her. Or at least not a language we recognise as connected to consciousness. We experience them as bodies whose actions and motivations we don't understand. We experience them, in other words, as madness, but also as death, because an animal is something that can die without explanation. It's perhaps true that we would be less mad ourselves, he said, if we had better relationships with animals, and that we would fear our own bodies less if we ceased to fear theirs. At least, he said to Julia, this challenge was not presented to you as a test of masculinity. It would be very difficult, as a man, to admit to the woman who rang your bell that you were incapable of getting rid of her pigeons for her.

I thought masculinity didn't exist any more, said Betsy flatly. I thought there was just violence. Anyway, she said to Thomas, there are plenty of people who are too afraid to kill themselves, even if they want to. That's because what they're actually afraid of is being alive.

I don't think of suicide as an act of courage, the director said thoughtfully. I suppose I was taught to think of it as the ultimate cowardice. But I was surprised to hear you describe yourself as a coward, she said to Thomas. It doesn't seem characteristic of you to admit a thing like that. I've always seen you as perfectly steady and strong.

Thomas gave his somewhat ghoulish smile. His baldness

revealed the bumps and articulations of his scalp, and the mechanism of his smile sent furrows all over the top of his head.

I was a little surprised myself, he said. But I seem to be doing a lot of things these days that are out of character. I am perhaps coming out of character, he said, like an actor does.

How did you meet? asked Julia, looking from one of them to the other.

We were at school together, the director said. We're both from the east, which means we would probably recognise each other even if we'd never met. Thomas is a teacher, she said, and I will never understand how he has managed to do something so unselfish with the second part of his life, given what the first part was.

Actually, Thomas said, I have just given up my job.

Have you really? the director said.

I resigned a few months ago, he said. I don't set my alarm clock any more. My bicycle stays in its shed. I don't spend the evening organising my papers and putting them in my satchel. And last month, he said, I didn't receive my paycheck.

And what are you going to do? asked Julia.

I don't know, Thomas said. I don't know what I will do or what I will be. For the first time in my life I am free. I saved up a little money, because of course that's the first thing anyone thinks of, but I find that even money has lost its power to coerce me. My father died not long ago, he said, and I made this decision almost the next day, quite naturally. With him gone, I immediately found that I no longer needed to play the part of myself. Perhaps I no longer need to exist at all.

I didn't know he had died, the director said sadly.

He died without having really lived, Thomas said, and while that kind of thing is easy to say, to witness the reality of it is quite shattering. You might say that he wasn't allowed to live by history and the politics of this country, but I always somehow believed that there was something human – a soul, if I can use that word – that would survive the worst attempts to crush it. But in fact nothing of him survived. When things changed, he didn't change – he walked around like a piece of the old reality that had somehow got left behind in the new one. My wife is a poet, he said, and my father never bothered to disguise the fact that he viewed her occupation as a frivolous waste of time. She grew up in the west, where the freedom to care about art and literature was what mattered, but for him that kind of thing was a luxury. I myself once wanted to be a writer, he said, but that ambition was basically unthinkable in my family, because our relationship to truth was so violent. People think that suffering and oppression are somehow nourishing to artists, he said, but I can tell you it isn't true. We are deformed emotionally and spiritually by oppression. My father was condemned to silence, and our family life was almost completely silent. Now that things here have changed, he said, a different kind of silence is emerging. Everyone wants to forget what happened, or perhaps they are just unable to remember. So this silence is a sort of oblivion, like the skin re-forming over a wound, where what happened doesn't matter any more. My wife and I have sometimes talked about this, he said, and occasionally even argued about it. There was a time when I suspected that she too would have preferred to forget about the past, because only then could other things start to matter. Only then could it seem important to write poetry.

If she's like most poets, Mauro said, she suspects that what she does is entirely useless, not because it's a luxury but in the sense that a spider's web hanging in the corner of a room is useless. Everyone ignores the spider's web, which nonetheless required enormous persistence and patience to make and yet can be brushed away in an instant without anyone noticing. No one notices poetry, he said, but when they find it and look closely at it they see something marvellous, like the spider's web. The spider's web has nothing to do with history or politics or oppression, he said, it exists in a different reality from those things and is obviously much weaker and more fragile than they are. It is more linked to survival than to power or violence – it survives in spite of them. It can be brushed away and all that work wasted, but then the work starts again, in another corner of the room.

Thomas stared at Mauro with his unblinking eyes.

I have always been the responsible and practical one in our relationship, he said presently. I went to work and let the spider make its web undisturbed. But increasingly I began to suspect that this responsibility and practicality had been foisted on me, not just by the impracticality of poetry but by all the unwritten codes that determine who is responsible for whom. At times, he said, I even found myself agreeing in my mind with my father in seeing my wife's position as indulgent. Why should poetry not pay its way, as everything else has to? Why should I be made unfree, so that she can express herself? It was extraordinarily painful for me to have these thoughts, he said, because I have always been proud of her work and proud of myself for supporting her. It has always felt like a definitive break from my past, he said, to live beside a creative person in this way. Obviously when I decided to leave my job we talked a great deal about the problems this would cause for her, and though I told her I wouldn't give it up without her agreement, I'm not sure that's actually true. She was very shocked at first, and troubled by her own reaction. We decided long ago not to have children, he said, but suddenly she began to say that she wished she did have a child. I think she thought that I would never leave my job if there was a child to support, whereas my obligation to support her was less clear. Some of these conversations, he said, came close to horror, as though we were admitting some devil's pact had been lying all along underneath the surface of our apparently peaceful and loving life. But eventually she agreed that I could leave my job, he said, and for a while she even talked about the opportunity it might offer for her to become braver and stronger.

There's no money to be made in poetry, he said, and so she needed to look for other things that she could do. She applied for jobs at magazines, and for editing jobs at publishing houses, but her lack of skills and experience meant that she was never chosen. She attended countless interviews, walking around and around the city until she was exhausted. She began to feel constantly unwell, an unspecific illness that nonetheless seemed to get worse every day. She used to feel quite happy in her life, he said, and satisfied by the work that she did, but with all these rejections she started to see herself as a failure. It was clear that she felt angry with me, he said, for putting her in this situation, and one day when she tripped in the road on the way to an interview and hurt herself quite badly, she became wildly upset, blaming me entirely for the fact that this had happened to her. Deep down I think she expected me to reverse my decision, he said, once I had seen how hard she had tried, but instead of going back to my teaching job I began to write a book, the book that I had had in my mind for many years. I was sorry for her, he said, but what was surprising was that I did not feel particularly guilty, despite the fact that I had always treated her as something precious that needed to be looked after. In one of our arguments, I finally admitted that I didn't know what the outcome of our situation would be. I didn't know what would come after responsibility, and after the ways of being that I had dutifully observed all my life. All I knew was that I couldn't go back to them. It was a leap, I told her, a leap into darkness and ignorance. She was so struck by this idea, he said, the idea that a person might have to fall for a while in order to change, that from that moment she began to think about things in a different way.

She started to ask herself why she had become a writer, he said, and especially why she had chosen so marginal a field, where – other than a few geniuses – one was unlikely to make a mark. She could not support herself by writing poetry, and nor did she believe that her poetry was essential to anyone. She found pleasure in writing it, of course, as others found pleasure in reading it, but she didn't believe it was a necessity to them. No, it was not a necessity, he said, and nor was it a practicality – in fact she detected something covert about it, something underhand in this taking of secret pleasure. Perhaps, after all, she wrote poetry because she was frightened of doing anything else, in other words precisely for its impracticality. And because she wanted to be a writer, a desire which after all was maybe only the product of her reverence for other writers. Then, by chance, a teacher friend invited her to come and talk to her class about poetry. This was the kind of thing that she always refused to do because it frightened her, but in this new mood of change she accepted. When she returned she was exhilarated: it had been wonderful, the freshness and enthusiasm of the young people, the unexpectedness of their thoughts, and most of all her own competence in running the class, for which of course she had been over-prepared. At a certain point the headteacher had come in to listen, and she asked my wife afterward whether she had ever considered a career in teaching. As of one month ago, he said, smiling, it is now my wife who packs her papers in her satchel in the evening and sets her alarm for the morning, while I go to my study to write. It is too soon of course to know, he said, whether this reversal of roles will be as happy an ending in reality as it is to my story, but for now it makes us laugh, he said, to have come up with it.

As long as you don't rub salt in the wound by writing a bestseller, Betsy said.

I know a lot of women who assume that the men they live with will be financially responsible for them, Julia said. It's true that usually they have children, and most of them talk about it as a deal they made at the beginning, but the deal is always the same, that the man will earn the money while the woman allows her career and her ambitions to take second place. Sometimes I have been jealous of these women, she said, because I live without a partner and support myself and my daughter, and to be able to live your life without considering every action in the light of practical necessity seems to me an almost unacceptable privilege. At other times I see that the absence of necessity weakens their ambitions, and that they allow themselves to become unprepared to survive alone. Their lives are so gendered, she said, it is almost as if they trust gender more than anything else to tell them how to live. One of the things that interests me about G's work, she said, is that she treats both sexes as doomed by gender, as almost interchangeable in that sense, so that a third sex emerges in which the man and the woman have merged into each other and become neutral. The couple, in other words, becomes a kind of two-headed monster with little children dangling from its sides. I know other couples of course who try to do things more equally, she said, and to preserve their separate identities, but they seem to have even more problems than the conventional ones, who at least present their family life as perfect. Some friends of mine have a small child, she said, and they agreed to share the responsibility to earn money with the responsibility to care for her. The woman spends half her time working and half her time with her daughter. But when it's the man's turn to care for the child, he employs a nanny to do his half. He claims that he has not reneged on their deal, which was to share the responsibility equally – the child is cared for by the nanny, who he alone pays. But it enrages the woman that he doesn't wish to be with the child as much as she does, and that while she is working she has to worry about whether the nanny is doing things right. They argue about it all the time, even in public, Julia said. The woman is so infuriated by what she sees as an injustice, and what he presents as a logical arrangement, that she has clearly come to hate him.

Overhead the dull black sky was mottled like a bruise with greenish light. People were leaving, and the tumult of voices had died down to a thick murmur. The golden lamps shed their glow in the emptying spaces. A feeling of pliancy, as though time had momentarily loosened its grip, seemed to emerge from the waning of urgency. Here and there the waiters stood talking in the shadows.

I should go home, the director said. This day has been so long and strange that I'm not sure how to make it end. But I suppose it will end like any other day.

Her narrow face was flushed. She looked physically spent but exhilarated, like an athlete at the end of a race. Only her small pale eyes held a light of fear and she closed them, a mysterious smile on her mouth.

I can go with you, Thomas said. We could walk together, if you aren't too tired. I feel like walking, he said. In the end I was too ugly for this restaurant, and only walking will restore my anonymity.

The director laughed.

I know what you mean, she said. I'd also like to walk. I feel like moving fast.

She groped around in her bag and brought out a bulging wallet of creased leather.

I'll leave the card with you, she said to Mauro and Julia. You can give it back to me tomorrow. Goodnight, the director said to the rest of us. Earlier today I didn't know what was going to happen, she said. I couldn't see how things were going to continue nor what course they could possibly take. Yet somehow the time has passed, or we have made it pass. I doubt I'll see most of you again, she said, but I'm grateful to have had your company.

Thank you for including me, Thomas said. Though I'm worried my contribution was too personal. I feel suspiciously lighter, he said, as if I'd given away a part of myself. I'm wondering now if what I said was actually true, he said doubtfully. Perhaps if I told my story again, it would be completely different.

He offered the director his arm and they turned to go, his huge form beside her small and narrow one, resuming their conversation in low voices that gradually became indistinct as they passed through the empty tables toward the darkness of the passageway.

Still, I wouldn't want to be in her shoes, Betsy said, observing them as they left. I doubt she's heard the end of it. Imagine if he'd fallen on top of someone.

I guess he looked down first, David said.

What, as if he was crossing the road? Betsy said.

How should I know? David said. I don't know what someone like that thinks.

I don't think you care to know, Betsy said. And nor should you.

David smiled, a thin lucid smile that seemed suddenly to illuminate his whole face.

You're right, he said. I don't care.

All the better for you, Betsy said. Caring is overrated.

I wish I did, David said.

Why, so that you could throw yourself over some railings too? Betsy said.

I guess so, David said, still smiling.

Like I said, people shouldn't care so much, Betsy said. They just become overwrought.

I have no reason to care, David said. I've never found a reason.

That's because life has treated you too kindly, Betsy said. You're fortune's favourite child. You're spoiled.

I don't hurt anyone, David said. I don't stop a woman writing poetry. I don't support a woman either, or prevent one from leaving her child. I never had to involve myself in things like that. I never wanted to.

That's true, Betsy said, and it's what stops you being intolerable. You're white and you're male and things just fall into your lap, and I'm not saying that's your fault. You didn't do anything to make it happen and you didn't stop it either. You just let yourself be carried along like a cork in the water, always floating on the top.

You got that from G, David said. It was what she used to say.

I probably did, Betsy said.

She never said it about me, David said. She said it about men who took their pleasure that way. She knew a lot of men like that. She never saw me in that light. I always expected her to but she never did. I think she was mistaken, he said. It's one of the few mistakes I saw her make. But I didn't take pleasure from my situation – I didn't take anything at all. So she never noticed.

Why should she notice? Betsy said. She liked having you around.

David was silent, looking down at his fingers gripping his wine glass as though they were acting of their own accord.

I always felt there was something more for her, he said, something I was standing in the way of. She liked me because she thought I resolved the dilemma of men for her. I stood outside the arena of family and biology. I wasn't her lover and I wasn't her son and maybe she didn't notice that even so I was still a man. Not much of a man, he said, but a man all the same. She never had a daughter, and sometimes I used to think that was what she thought I was. But she was wrong.

Maybe a daughter would have made her disappear, Mauro said. Maybe she had to be the only woman. And of course she always remained a daughter herself.

Do you think she would have overcome her dislike of women if she had had a female child? Julia asked David.

She didn't hate women, David said. She was afraid of them. She used men to protect her from women.

But in that case they were also protecting her from herself, Julia said.

Maybe, David said.

There are plenty of men who are afraid of men, Mauro said.

149

With good reason, Betsy said. In G's case I think the fear was a fear of caste. I don't think she objected to women, especially not powerful women, but she didn't want to be recognised as one, by them or by anyone else.

You said she had never loved, Julia said to David. Do you mean that she missed the opportunity to love women?

She could have loved herself, David said.

Except that she despised that idea, Betsy said.

She thought it was a form of weakness, David said. She thought it would distract her from reality. At the end she wanted me with her all the time, he said. I felt I was deceiving her. She used to say she found peace with me. My passivity was restful to her, but it didn't mean anything. It had no meaning at all. I thought she could have found something better. She had awful dreams, David said. At the end her dreams were harrowing. She used to tell me about them because she couldn't contain them. She dreamed disgusting things about her own body, that she had plants or weeds growing out of her skin, that her legs were covered with fish-scales. Often her dreams took place in a kind of decaying underworld or hell where people chastised or menaced her. These dreams were like sewage. Her dead parents walked through them like zombies, she would find her dead husband in dark corners committing acts of sadism. She was ashamed that her mind was producing these dreams. Often, he said, she dreamed she had daughters. In the dreams she was never at home with the daughters – they were always in strange places, foreign cities or unfamiliar houses, trying to get somewhere or dealing with threatening situations. Often she would fail to protect them or she would lose them and not be able to find them. She would go mad with anxiety and guilt, trying to get to them. In one dream they were waiting for a train, but when it came they couldn't get on. They were in a huge flat landscape in the middle of nowhere. She decided they should walk, and so they walked along narrow roads with cars passing, until they came to the place they were trying to get to. It was an enormous house full of empty rooms and there were strange people there who misled her or distracted her. She didn't even realise she had lost her daughters until the morning, when they came and found her. They were weeping, and there was something so fresh and vivid in their weeping, something so true and alive, that she almost burst with the most agonising feeling of love for them. They wept and then they told her that while they were out of her sight they had been raped all night by their father. She went to find this man, full of horror and fury. She found him asleep in a strange room and she woke him up. He was a composite of all the men she had known. She asked him if it was true and eventually he admitted it was. This dream, David said, nearly broke her apart. She couldn't survive it, the admission of the man and the pain of the daughters and between them her own failure. I guess I'm betraying her, he said. I never did betray her until now.

Well, then don't, Betsy said. It wouldn't hurt you to have to keep a few secrets. It'd be good for your character.

She gave me her dreams, David said. Without knowing enough about me. I don't know enough about myself to own her dreams. I'm haunted by them, he said. There's nowhere for me to put them.

Maybe the joke is on you, Betsy said. Maybe that was her parting gift to the male sex, to install a man with her nightmares. I may sleep better myself on that thought, she said, gathering her handbag. It feels like it's time to call a taxi. Let's hope they've finished their cleaning-up operation out there by now.

Yes, it's late, Julia said. Mauro, we should ask for the bill.

David stood up heavily and went to help Betsy out of her chair. She struggled briefly, leaning on his arm and giving great puffs of effort.

I'm there, she said triumphantly once she was on her feet. I don't know how you stay so steady, she said to David, considering the amount you drink, but you're as sturdy as a tree.

I think we've agreed that's my fate, David said.

Well, goodbye, Betsy said, while everyone rose to say farewell. I hope we'll meet again. What's the expression they have in this country? If it only happened once, it didn't happen at all.

They slowly made their way across the courtyard, Betsy limping and David walking very slowly and upright beside her while she clutched his arm. Mauro and Julia went inside with the director's card to pay the bill. A few people were left around the tables and their elongated shadows and the shadows of the ornamental trees made outlandish silhouettes against the walls. The waiters had cleared everything away and the tables stood bare of their linen. From inside the building the distant clattering of plates and saucepans could be heard. A red light pulsed faintly and mysteriously in the sky overhead. We waited for Mauro and Julia to come back.

The Spy

Not long ago our mother died, or at least her body did – the rest of her remained obstinately alive. She took a considerable time to die and outlasted the nurses' predictions by many days, so that those of us who had been summoned to her bedside had to depart again and return to our lives.

No one cried at her death, though among the congregation at the funeral there were some outbursts of shocked weeping, as though at the sight of death being surprised in the act of stealing from life. It was the entrance of the coffin, rather than the death itself, that constituted the violence of this act. The coffin was shocking, and this must always be the case, whether or not one disliked being confined to the facts as much as our mother had. The body inside the coffin was entirely factual. She had never seemed to take much notice of her body: it had been her vehicle, that was all. But its authority, it turned out, had been absolute.

For a while afterward there was a feeling of lightness, a feeling almost of freedom. The violence of death had the appearance of a strange generosity. A capital sum had been returned to the living: we on the side of life had been in some way increased. But in fact an unease remained which grew and which was our mother's impenetrable bequest to us. There ought to have been a feeling not of freedom but of loss. If there was loss, then it was of something we had never had. We were free simply from the conundrum of this double loss.

It was noted that at the funeral we had remained unmoved. It was a day of extreme, almost frightening heat, like the day of Meursault's mother's funeral at the beginning of Camus' *L'Étranger*. Meursault's own seeming indifference that day was also noted: it later became a central piece of evidence in his trial and conviction as a heartless killer. Was our indifference likewise a philosophical refutation of the social contract? Had we too run the risk of being arrested and convicted for the failure to adhere to cultural and moral norms?

Months later, at dawn on the ninth floor of a hotel in a northern city, standing before a view of astonishing ugliness, it became evident that our mother was accompanying us in a way she had not when she was alive. Far below, people scurried across the concrete spaces in the cold grey morning. A violent wind was blowing. It shook the power lines and the leafless trees. It rattled the hoardings outside the shopfronts. It upended the litter bins and sent their contents whirling madly into the air.

The mother of the film-maker G did not know who her son was: his name, which had become widely known, was not in fact his real name. He had assumed it so that she should not discover what he did. While she lived she knew nothing of his illustrious career, and even after she died he maintained this alias and the habits of secrecy and disguise that came with it.

His films were naturalistic and poetic, and his mother might not in fact have found much in them to disapprove of, but he would not have been able to create them in the guise of himself. Yet what was perhaps most unusual about them was that they were always instantly recognisable as his. His style, so uninterfering, drew attention to itself without meaning to. He rarely, for instance, showed his characters in close-up, believing that this was not how human beings saw one another. His films had no particular aesthetic. They often took place in public spaces, and his characters seemed barely to notice that they were being watched. They wore ordinary clothes and rarely looked at the camera. They were absorbed in their own lives.

For those accustomed to the camera's penetration of social and physical boundaries and the strange authority of its prying eye, this absence of what might be called leadership was noticeable. People were often baffled or even angered by his films. They expected a storyteller to demonstrate his mastery and control by resolving the confusion and ambiguity of reality, not deepening it. Even the more radical film-makers among G's contemporaries at least gained respect through the boldness and assertiveness of their artistic vision.

G's parents lived in a large house in a bourgeois country town, and this is where G had spent his childhood. There were four children, of whom G was the eldest, a position that entailed the maximum exposure to the parents and their customs and beliefs. Like the figurehead on the prow of a boat, G had received the first impact of their natures, to which the momentum of youth imparted a continuous quality of violence. This violence was societal rather than personal, for his parents were people of strict conventionality and religion. Later he saw himself as a door between them and the whole notion of inner life, and his discovery that this door could be kept shut was both relieving and fateful. The other children used this barrier he had created to free themselves from certain inhibitions and constraints. Later they claimed to have been greatly marked by the parental regime, and it was in their ability to make this claim that the difference between them and G lay.

G left the town as soon as he could, going away to study and then finding work as a teacher in another region. He had expected to find sympathy among children. His own childhood appeared to qualify him for that sphere, as though this were his expertise. His ambition, so long held that it had the character of an assumption, was to be a writer, and it had seemed to him that teaching would naturally fit with that goal. But in fact there could have been nothing worse than to encumber himself with the obligation to form and control children. One day he simply abandoned his post, telling no one except his brother, and for many years afterward his parents continued to believe that he was a schoolteacher.

The brother lived in the city now, where he was distinguishing himself in academic and philosophical circles. G went to stay with him: they went to cafes and restaurants and jazz clubs where G met his friends and associates, clever young men who played with language like indefatigable athletes. Their sport was to take a precept that had functioned eternally as a pillar of reality and demolish it: reality did not generally, as a consequence, come tumbling down, but one's sense of its solidity and familiarity was altered. Obtuse with innocence, blinkered by a lifetime of dissimulation before authority, G was slow to realise that these men – including his brother – were homosexual. The brother talked openly, even obsessively,

about the privations of his childhood and the deform-
ation of body and mind that was the result of having had
to conceal his true nature. He wrote philosophical articles advocating for the sexual liberation of children and
published them under his own name. G did not discuss
these articles with his brother, and was generally silent in
the company of his brother's friends. He found that he
hid from their upending of conventionality much as he
had always hidden from its enforcement. But he decided
not to return to the town where he had been living.
He found an apartment of his own in the city. Alone for
the first time in his life, he looked out of the window day
after day at the rooftops and sky and tried to consider
what he would do.

The view from our window is of rooftops and sky, and
of other top-floor windows set at angles determined by
the pattern of the streets below. The emptiness between
the buildings is thus shaped according to the same pattern. This elevated world, with its streets of air, seems
to suspend the humans who live up here in another element: the windows are a kind of lens through which they
become representational. The building opposite has a little round window in its mansard roof, and sometimes the
face of a small girl appears there. When she notices that
she is being watched she waves, as though from one boat

to another. Often people open their windows and lean out, looking down and around. Being seen while seeing, they are doubly illuminated by the light of perception. At sunrise, across the void in the quiet of morning, a man appears on the balcony opposite to smoke, the lower half of his body wrapped in a towel. He is young and bronze-chested. He lights his cigarette and looks at his phone while the pink light fills all the windows behind him. His freedom in that moment seems absolute.

At night, when the lights are on, the scenes playing high up in the windows are framed by the emptiness, like paintings. They are paintings of people in rooms, together or alone, seen through windows or across spaces by an eye that seems larger and more omniscient than a human eye. It could be the eye of a god, or equally that of an animal or a child. The human figures have a theatrical quality: in the recurrence of their own lives they seem to exist outside time. That quality in the view from our window arises not because the people are consciously enacting themselves, but because perception itself – the pure perception that involves no interaction, no subjectivity – reveals the pathos of identity.

Does it help people to be seen, even when they don't know it? A mother is continually seen by her children, whether or not she credits them with a point of view. From the beginning they are amassing images of her, of her body in all its angles and positions and moods. Her body becomes the known point from which they broach all that is unknown. They see her mainly when she is paying them no attention; when her attention comes it is seismic, as though the actor has suddenly turned and addressed a member of the audience. They see her when she thinks she is alone, despite the fact that they are there. These witnesses that have grown out of her can startle or displease her with the independence of their observations. They are not the extensions of her own will and consciousness that she had believed them to be. In this way they inform her that she cannot control what is known about her and does not entirely know herself. They know more about her than she does about them, since they have not yet become fully themselves. Yet her power to wound them is limitless.

She had had many pregnancies, and had become steadily debilitated by excess weight and sedentary habits. She seemed to want and welcome debility: perhaps it was a way of drawing attention to the site of contention that was her body. Her personality, so dominant, was as though clad in the statement of its own ultimate disempowerment. She offered her flesh as another person might offer their beauty. This flesh was a sort of outcome, the result of all the things that had been done to her body during her life, whether by herself or others. Inexorably, year by year, she lost her shape. Her formlessness became a sort of challenge to the notion of form itself and to conformity. She discovered that she could use this non-conformity to control what people expected her to do and therefore what they were able to do themselves. In this sense her formlessness was the active counterpart of her beauty. When she had possessed beauty, her management of outcomes had been far less successful. In formlessness she discovered power, and also a freedom from limitation.

She laid claim to all kinds of maladies, had unnecessary operations and took all the drugs the doctors were willing to prescribe her; she insisted on using a wheelchair, and eventually refused to walk at all. When she said she had cancer no one believed her: it is possible she didn't believe it herself. But finally, one day, a doctor confirmed it. He told her she would shortly die, and her response to this news at first was as to the fulfilment of a fantasy of attention or importance, as though she had at last been offered the starring role she had always felt was destined for her. The encounter with reality, deferred for so long, avoided by so many ruses and fictions, proved in the end hard to recognise. She mistook death for a compliment, and when finally she realised that this dark stranger was not a prince but an assassin, she struggled vainly to get away. She tried to walk: the news reached us that after all these years of half-voluntary paralysis she was attempting to get out of her wheelchair and walk. It seemed she thought that she could simply stop playing, stop pretending – that she could reverse her will and take refuge in reality. But for her there was no longer any reality: she had long since broken her contract with it. She had allowed it to decay all around her, in her pursuit of limitlessness.

Some weeks after she died she entered our dream, walking through it without seeming to see it or know she was there. She was giant and doll-like, an inflated unclothed figure moving robotically forward as though in a trance. The people in the dream moved out of the way to let her pass. She saw nothing and nobody, walking mechanically past them and away, walking naked out of the dream as she had walked into it, as though her fate was to walk and walk in this monstrous fashion for eternity. When she passed us she showed no recognition. We looked at her face and felt a leap of consternation and pity. It was her true face, the one we had never seen but had somehow known about and imagined since childhood. It wore an expression of unspeakable unhappiness.

Alone in the city for days at a time, G wrote a novel. It concerned the lives of young people in a bourgeois country town over the course of one summer. These young people were paralysed by the disconnection between their inner and outer lives and by the difficulty of locating authenticity in their own feelings. They lived in comfortable households and spent their time engaged in pleasant summer activities, but their glimpses of the moral and natural beauty of the world only made their attempts to relate to one another seem ugly and false. The coupling instinct, with its flirtations and ellipses and its adherence to the narrative framework of romance, felt artificial and constraining. Yet in fact it was this marriage of instinct and narrative that would eventually drive them into social conformity. The youthful truth of their feelings, along with their bonds to nature and spirituality, would be lost.

A publisher bought the novel, which came out under an assumed name. G had made up this name midway through his writing process, when it became clear to him that he was unable to write freely as himself. The prospect of being identified with his own actions plunged him into the same dilemma as that of his characters: the loss of an internal truth through the construction of external identity. There was shame and inhibition, too, at the idea of the people who knew him – his parents above all – having this open access to his private world. Even the thought of it was intolerable.

The use of an alias was undeniably cowardly. By

contrast his brother seemed to relish his open confrontation with their childhood world and its conservative
perspectives. Why should families go unchallenged by
the reality that comes to them through their children?
The whole question of authority, and the institutions
that embodied it, was changing. His brother had been
awarded a professorship at the city's most illustrious uni-
versity. Who was to tell him what he could and couldn't
think? But for G there was a question of responsibility
that his brother seemed content to ignore. To challenge,
to inflict, was also to entail responsibility. His fear of
inflicting and causing almost amounted to an aesthetic
and moral objection to the phenomenon of causation.
Yet his use of an alias had the appearance of a criminal
luxury, to the extent that it could have been said to be
a form of cheating. To conceal identity is to take from
the world, without paying the costs of self-declaration.
When his novel failed to attract any attention, he wondered whether it was a punishment for this crime.

In the city he began to meet artists and writers and
film-makers, young people caught up in the dynamism of
remaking culture for the modern era. Like his brother's,
their ambitions involved a confrontation with conformity, but in this case they were focused on redefining
the relationship between art and reality. Some of them
were already becoming famous, and he watched as their

identities grew inextricably intertwined with their creations. When they brought out something new, it was compared to the last thing they had done; it was praised or criticised on that basis; a familiarity, a form of ownership had been established that permitted judgement. Why was it impossible to create without identity? Why did a work need to be identified with a person, when it was just as much the product of shared experience and history? Some of his friends became bolder and more arrogant with success. Their voices grew louder, their opinions and convictions began to entail a kind of deafness. Watching them, G felt a curious sense of isolation, as though he alone could see and hear. In being and defending themselves, they cloaked the world in their subjectivity. He began to understand that the discipline of concealment yielded a rare power of observation. The spy sees more clearly and objectively than others, because he has freed himself from need: the needs of the self in its construction by and participation in experience.

Meanwhile G and a few others had set up a magazine, where G wrote film reviews under another assumed name. It was unlikely his parents would ever hear of these reviews, but all the same he knew they would have disapproved of them. His was the opposite of his brother's attempt to heal the self by seeking the root causes of its unhappiness. It was, in a sense, an ultimate autonomy.

Yet his disguise seemed to lie beyond the preserve of either love or freedom. Rather, there was something theatrical, something almost godlike about it. It was both humble and divine, this management of the power of disturbance, born of his deep habits of deception or of the obligation to deceive. The humble god who avoids violence and is bent on the preservation of things as they are: this was the god he wished to recognise. In the service of that preservation, sovereign identity must be dethroned. Invisibility was his conduit to self-expression, though it had done nothing so far but consign his work to oblivion. But while he was invisible he was free.

His reviews began to attract notice for their striking avoidance of the word 'I'. The memory of his novel now embarrassed him: his idea of writing had begun to falter. Of all the arts, it was the most resistant to dissociation from the self. A novel was a voice, and a voice had to belong to someone. In the shared economy of language, everything had to be explained; every statement, even the most simple, was a function of personality. He remembered how exposed he had felt as a child, as his mother steadily built a panorama of cause and effect around him. He was publicly identified with everything he did and said, as well as with what he did not do or say. Writing seemed a drastic enlargement of this predicament.

He wrote a collection of stories, little morality tales for the modern era, or so he thought them. They concerned ordinary people in moments of intimate dilemma. They revealed – so he thought – all the simple beauty of the self, faced by the problem of truth. Instead of directing his characters he merely watched them, without inter-fering, like the humble kind of god. He watched them lovingly, for the good and the bad in them. He brought them no drama. He forced nothing on them, extended as they already were by the task of living. The things that happened to them and the choices they made could always, he found, be connected to them in a unique way, not by any external factor but by something much finer and more delicate, something more in the way of a com-pass inside each one of them. He was adept at sensing the minutest tremors of this compass. His publisher rejected the stories. What's happened to you? the pub-lisher said exasperatedly, when G came to his office. You were modern when you started, and now you've gone back into the last century!

We resumed our lives after the funeral as though noth-ing had occurred. There was the feeling that something had stopped and something else had begun, but neither state had any clear definition. They were empty spaces with no content or language. There was the feeling that they ought to have been full with the knowledge of possession and loss. Sometimes we were arrested by the sensation that we were now alone in the world but how could that be? If it were so, then we had always been alone.

She had liked us best when we were small children, before our will and character began to obstruct her will and character. Once, she said that what she had in fact liked best was being pregnant. In pregnancy she had received attention for what was as yet a swelling mystery, one that also had the advantage of excusing her from the requirements and obligations of normality. This attractive prospect, like an interest-free loan, may have been what tempted her to repeat the exercise so often, even – or especially – when its pitfalls were before her eyes. But pregnancy is not a sustainable state: perhaps her discovery that she disliked reality and its logic was made there. Pregnancy was a reverse kind of authorship, where the work started after publication and the suspension of disbelief came before the story had begun. She was creating, sure enough, but what a troublesome creation it turned out to be, leaving her no peace, disobeying her intentions and, most of all, proving impossible to put an end to. Pregnancy concluded with the drama of birth. Love ended with the spectacle of marriage. But we didn't end, not even with our own marriages, our own births.

She wanted us to be finished but we could never be finished. We kept existing and ruining the order of things. We got into trouble for existing in this way. Her anger was easily aroused by disobedience and contradiction. Nothing we did wrong could be forgotten, and so as we grew older we felt more and more uncomfortably weighed down by our characters, which seemed to have been imposed on us. Her ambitions for us were uncomfortable and didn't seem to fit us. We were embarrassed by the story she had fashioned for us and the roles we had been given. We discovered that for the story to work, a great deal of licence had to be taken with the truth. The strange feeling of liberation at her death was in fact our liberation from this story. But why had she created it?

When we became adolescents, and started to query her version of our life, she did something unusual: she began to make up new stories about the time that pre-dated our existence. It is the strategy of dictators, to rewrite history. Was this what she was? The stories concerned herself and her life before she met our father. It was easy enough to discount them by a simple calculation of dates, but this only seemed to increase their maddening power. In one of these stories there had been another suitor, before our father. Unlike our father this suitor was rich, aristocratic and charming, with connections to high society, and he had wanted ardently to marry her. His parents disapproved, and sent him away for a year to the colonies, from where he promised he would write. But no letter came: for a whole year she waited, pining, for word from him. Then one day, looking in her sister's room for a missing blouse – the sister was always taking her things – she found a shoebox of letters under the bed. All these months the sister had waited jealously for the postman and intercepted the letters, which had arrived diligently every week. In the last letter he declared himself to be giving up hope, not having heard from her in all this time.

Another story – or rather set of stories – concerned her employment as an assistant to a certain wealthy *homme du monde* who travelled around the fashionable watering holes of Europe among a coterie of celebrated artists and intellectuals of the day. These stories had more the character of an inexhaustible series. She found that she could lay claim, through this man, to a familiarity with a whole range of people and places, and to having participated in some of the key cultural moments of the era. Mixing in these circles eventually led to the discovery that she herself possessed artistic talent, and with her employer's encouragement she enrolled at the Chelsea School of Art. Later it became the Slade School of Fine Art, when she realised the Chelsea wasn't as well regarded. She generally stopped short of claiming outright that our father had put an end to these roman-tic and artistic adventures. Just before she died, she told him that she hated him.

We lived in our bodies as in a constant state of emer-gency. We wore them out trying to either satisfy or exhaust them. We never succeeded in losing ourselves in sleep or pleasure. We were vigilant and wakeful. We always knew what time it was. We were forever trying to fill or close some gap and it gradually became clear that she was the origin of it, of this unbreachable distance within ourselves; perhaps it was in fact the gap between her body and ours that tormented us.

We had considered neither language nor silence in relation to this gap. They were irrelevant to it, did not belong to it. In fact they belonged to her: she used them both as instruments of terror. The death of her body promised their liberation. It was strange to consider that, while the gap in our bodies would remain unresolved, we might avail ourselves of language and silence. There had been no silence that was not an aggression, no language that was not an attempt to exert judgement and con-trol. Silence had filled us with the panic of abandonment; language had seemed a kind of evil, capable of destabilis-ing reality. One day they might become innocent again. With her body gone, what would we say or not say?

For many years love remained a mystery to us and

in its place we practised concealment. Everything that we cared about and desired had to be hidden. We did not know that outside in the world this element, love, encompassed all that was freely available to us. Instead, when it was offered we spurned it. We were suspicious of those who lived in love, who gave and expected nothing in return. Sometimes we encountered the shocking faces of reality – suffering, injustice, pain and loss – and wondered in our hearts how such things could possibly be borne. Our bankruptcy in love left us with no ability to bear them. Yet she – and we – were largely spared reckonings of this kind. Misfortune never knocked at her door, demanding payment. Catastrophe never came for her. She was never checked by reality, and this gave more power to her unreality. She disliked and was suspicious of the sufferings of others: they detracted attention from herself. She disliked the spirit of exploration. She disliked freedom, and bequeathed this dislike to us. She disliked all threats to her subjectivity. Most of all she scorned the truth, taunted and baited it and laughed in its face, and not until the very end, when death came and waited by her bed, did the truth act to defend itself.

Someone gave G an old film camera and looking through the lens he recognised this as his home. Its unbodied mode of perception – even if it was to some extent an illusion – furnished him with a hiding place. When he was behind the camera, he believed he could not be seen.

His years of watching films and writing about them had given him a tetchy sort of autonomy. He knew what other directors had done and were doing, what they were likely to do. He was familiar with the brutal grandeur of the highest achievements, the epoch-making spectacles of genius in this new and violently meaningful form, which married personal vision with extraordinary public impact and power. He knew that it embodied change, and he wasn't interested in change. He was interested in the fragments that change leaves behind in its storming passage toward the future.

His writing had been a failure but it had garnered him a quiet authority, because the proponents of change – the brutal geniuses – are susceptible to the notion of a seer in their midst. These men of power were surprisingly attentive to what G had to say. They wanted his approval, while completely ignoring his opinions, which were not the opinions of the majority. He posed no threat to them, with his austere and threadbare vision of life. But they recognised his connection to the truth.

His first attempt at making a film was a disaster. He was unprepared for the practical complexity of it, its tedium, its sprawling technical reality. He irritated the people whose help he needed, the crews and technicians of whose importance he had been arrogantly unconvinced. He was at once controlling and incompetent. There was an occasion when he himself was unable to find the location specified for that day's filming and everyone sat there waiting for all the hours marked on the call sheet. The simplicity of writing, its humble mode of transferring vision, was immeasurably distant from this strange and cumbersome process of recording. It seemed to go against the force of gravity – all these people, all this equipment, all this expense that was required to get his conception airborne. It directly contravened his nature and his view of life. He failed to comprehend its organisational basis and its reliance on time and location. He failed to accept that there was no place for daydreaming, hazarding, grasping. The gleaming prospect of invisible authorship had been replaced by a monstrous task of practical management.

Yet he did not return to writing: he was forced to recognise that the last thing he wanted to do was sit alone in a room. It was what he had always imagined for himself but still, he was unable to do it – a double failure. What was he trying to capture? What ineluctable vision that writing was so far from being able to comprehend? The statement of writing was already too crass, too formulated for this vision. The writer writes about what he already knows and has decided is there. He pretends he doesn't know, hasn't decided. He sells this illusion to the reader, who joins him in the labour of fantasy. G's conception was the opposite of this. He wanted to be innocent of knowledge. He wanted simply to record.

One day, for no tangible reason, he suddenly understood something: what he hated and resisted about film-making – its boring practicality – was the key to his vision. His religious upbringing had left him with some suspicious notions about suffering and divine intention. But the more he considered it, the more he realised that this was not the redemption that comes from doing what is hardest. No, it was by taking responsibility – something he had never done – that he would be redeemed. Other people were redeemed in this way by having children and by the task of caring for them. In a sense this offered the equivalent prospect of an advance into the mechanics of reality, by comparison with which the notion of sitting alone in a room writing a book seemed entirely pallid. It was easy, as a writer, to hide behind a pseudonym. But to go out into the world anonymously and record reality was a matter of enormous difficulty.

It interested him that actors pretended that the camera, the audience, was not there. Perhaps people pretended God wasn't there in much the same way. The sense of being seen was fundamental to the construction of civilised behaviour, to the extent that most people continued to behave in that way even when they were alone. Why did they? If not the eye of God, was it simply the gaze of authority they felt upon them? He, on the other hand, had no feeling of being seen. On the contrary, he was surprised – horrified even – when people noticed things about him. The gaze of authority had fallen on him so early that he had learned to put on a mask. But from the very beginning he had been aware of seeing as a type of power. To see without being seen: for G there was no better definition of the artist's vocation.

He decided to do things his own way. He would assemble a cast of people – they didn't need to be professional actors – and tell them what he had in mind. He would leave it to them to decide what they were going to do and say. He would only use available light, which meant, he supposed, that most of it would have to be shot outside. He would shoot the whole thing in a day, maybe two. If possible, he wouldn't alter what he had shot. He considered the places where people gathered and were seen: the street, the park, the beach. He would use those places. The biggest problem, he supposed, would be the weather.

His thoughts returned to the stories he had written years earlier, the stories of young people in moments of dilemma and illumination. These stories, he realised, were the template for his vision. Just as they had seemed to come from life, so he felt certain he could recreate them as true experiences. It was no wonder the publisher had rejected them. They needed to be animated by all the tender unknowing of life itself. He didn't want to direct them: he wanted to watch them happen.

The thrift and simplicity of G's method made it possible for him to create not just one film but a whole series. No single one of them distinguished itself or made any noise. They flowed quietly out into the world and seemed naturally to join the stream of life. In each one, a situation developed that had no clear beginning or end. It emerged and flowered and receded again over a day or a handful of days. He was old enough now to know that these situations, these flowerings, which in youth seem almost incidental to the forward-driving story of life, in fact turn out to be life itself. It was in these moments of hope and expectation and disillusion, of prelude, before the will decides to conscript the self into conformity, that we really lived.

It was noted that G's films usually revolved around the attempt by a young woman to remain free and truthful in the face of the deception and possessiveness of men. It astonished him to watch, over and over, the way his actors quite naturally found the language – the moral terms – for this struggle. The young women knew in their hearts that the freedom they wanted was not, in the end, available to them. And in fact the men who did understand their need to be free were not the men they desired.

With these little homespun tragedies G began to make his mark. But even when success came he kept to his methods and to his secrecy. No one knew anything about his life, his real name, his marriage and children, his connection to his notorious brother. No one knew what he wanted or why he was motivated to work in the way that he did. All they knew was what he saw.

Suddenly we could not tolerate capitalism. We found its presence in our lives, of which it had insidiously made a prison, repellent. Was our mother a function of capitalism?

We had relied from the beginning on the manufacture of desire to camouflage the problems of truth and limitation. Was there anything we remembered from the time before this reliance? Only fragments. Our mouths and bodies craved sensation. There was a terrible tension in the distance between our needs and their satisfaction. We made the discovery that we could create needs that we ourselves could satisfy. Later we found that our will could enlarge the possibilities of this cycle, whose end result was never the transformation of our circumstances but the rendering of them more tolerable. Slowly we understood that need had a crippling effect: it made us inflexible and secretive. Our bodies felt unacceptable and cumbersome to us, as though they were a burden we would have to carry forever. Sometimes it felt as though only with the removal of this burden would we be free. There appeared to be some primary necessity we lacked and were therefore always in pursuit of. If this was so, its substance remained a mystery. We were tormented by something no one else could see. Yet, far from causing us to flee, this torment seemed to cement us more and more where we stood.

When it came to love, we found ourselves confronting a foreign language. We did not know how to estimate or value things that were free. The things that were free – sex, conversation, the smell of grass in summer – unsettled us. We sought to commodify them and create outcomes from them. But they seemed to belong to everybody: we couldn't keep them for ourselves. So when the personal offer of love came, a specific love for us alone, it was irresistible. To the question, Is this what you want?, there was only one answer: yes. To be given something for free was unparalleled in our experience. How could we refuse it? In the system of love, we soon came to understand, all the things that were free retained their appearance of freedom while in fact being conscripted into ownership. Was love itself a system of ownership? Often we received the confusing impression that love disliked freedom and at the same time sought to impersonate it. But in this foreign language we could never be sure.

Using the system of love, we built a structure of possession. Our feelings lived in this structure and sought to replicate themselves there. They sought familiarity and the feeling of things being real. They sought repetition. Some of these feelings were presentable enough to show in public; others were left to roam the attics and cellars. We had the sense of our lives as a story: this had been the case for some time. According to this story the past was a place of unenlightenment from which we were continually in the process of delivering ourselves into the future. Our habits of need and satisfaction had given us an interest in the future. The future enlarged the prospects of satisfaction and embroidered the sense of desire. We had visions of it that we described in words. We were continually creating it, making our way to it, yet we never arrived there. Often the present moment – the bridge to the future – weakened and collapsed while we were inside it. Then we had to start building again. This interest in the future strongly resembled belief. The people who lived around us and perhaps loved us were struck by the strength of our belief. They listened to our visions of the future and sometimes participated in them. But they tired more quickly than we did of the effort it took to get there. They were more interested than us in the past and felt nostalgia for it. The present moment did not collapse under them: it was strengthened by this element – love – that we did not entirely understand. We tried to be loving but when the sound of footfall from the attics and cellars was loud in our ears we grew impatient with love. We wanted to move forward, into the future.

We acquired things and used them and disposed of them. What we liked best was disposing of them. It felt like disposing of the bad and burdensome parts of ourselves. It felt, momentarily, like disposing of our own bodies. Sometimes we sensed that we were living counter to nature, were at odds with it, and this manifested itself as an intolerable feeling of material chaos and disorder, to which a material solution could usually be found. We felt both exposed by and imprisoned in what we had built and the story we had created. We wondered, very occasionally, who we were. We looked at our mother and felt, dimly, that we were nothing but a response to her character. When we saw her, the relief afterward of getting away from her was dizzying: in those first moments the possibilities of freedom rose before us, as though all along there had been something we had, some alternative to ourselves, that we had failed to notice. But after a while a cold feeling of neglect would begin to grow in us. Without her scrutiny our lives felt unreal.

When we had children of our own, an era dawned that at first seemed to be characterised by results. Our children – the result of us – were not what we expected. From the beginning they seemed to know more than us. They seemed to contain some miracle, the spark of life, that we had never perceived in ourselves. We took their side – against what we weren't quite sure – without question. We were proud of our results. We did not need to dispose of them. We did not need them to end. We lost some of our interest in the future: a day became the sum total of its parts. In fact, our children seemed already to contain the future, and as our knowledge of them grew it became clear that it was knowledge of what already existed. How was our mother going to respond to these new allegiances? We believed that she too would learn from our children and profit from their miraculous wisdom. But when we offered our children to our mother, we were surprised by the judgements she made of them. She preferred one of them to another; she saw flaws in them, and compared their relative merits. She was not, as we were, transformed by them: in fact she made the suggestion that our management of them was inadequate, that we were ruining them, and with this, her first major tactical error, her power over us was suddenly broken.

Our children taught us how to love, and slowly we began to understand the extent of what we ourselves had not received. We began, for the first time, to love one other. We loved one other with the simple love of children, which had returned to us from the time before the beginning, the time we couldn't remember, the time before our reliance on satisfaction and need. Capitalism, whose only interest in love lay in its commodification within the system of possession, was not increased by this development. Our mother, too, disliked the new bonds of love that were growing among us. She tried to disrupt them, but we found that this simple love could resolve the misunderstandings that arose from her interference. We began to talk about the past, and discovered that our accounts of it were all different yet in some sense the same. Slowly, falteringly, a picture emerged. Sensing rebellion, our mother resorted to harsher tactics. Some of us were more susceptible to her control, others less so. On the latter she simply turned her back. For the first time we recognised ourselves as fit to judge her, for now we understood what it would be, to turn your back on your child. We knew that we would be incapable of turning our back on our children. For the first time, an incapacity had the weight of riches.

There is the suspicion that the products of capitalism are intended not to last. Our mother's lifetime was the lifetime of capitalism. Was she herself a commodity?

G returned home to the bedside of his mother, who was seriously ill. He had been busy with work and it had been longer than usual since he had visited. Thus it seemed to be his fault, the desiccated body on the bed, as white and light as the brittle seed casings that whirled down from the sycamore tree outside the window. Only her breathing, noisy and laboured, distinguished her. His father was behaving erratically. He stood at the foot of the bed and, raising his voice in command, ordered her to get up and make the lunch. She didn't hear him, didn't get up. The father was unable to look after another human being. He was unable to communicate in any way other than by giving orders.

G went into the town by bicycle to get medicines. The town was more or less the same as it had been in his youth, except that now it was full of cars. G hated cars with a passionate hatred. He refused to get in them, even taxis. It wasn't just their ugliness and the filth they spilled out that repelled him: they were humanity's decisive step in its move away from nature. He credited them with the power to destroy self-control, sensuality, intimacy itself. He also saw that with this development his own future as a chronicler had been threatened. He would be left behind, by people in cars. His characters, spiritual and actual pedestrians, would be drowned out in the noise and dust.

He sat by his mother's bedside and stroked her bony forehead and her thin, silken white hair. Her eyes were closed. He could look at her for as long as he liked: for the first time in his life, there was nothing to stop him. He wandered around and around her face as though it were some government building that had finally been opened to the public. She and his father had presented themselves to their children as part of a greater authority whose machinations were impersonal. He wondered what their true feelings were and whether they had ever had access to a sense of self in their serving of these ideals and regulations. So it surprised him when his father said, over the lunch G had to make for him, that he blamed G's brother for the mother's perilous state. Not long ago the brother had published a barely veiled account of their childhood. It depicted the parents as a regime, a far crueller and more culpable one than in G's vision, one that actually set out to crush and incapacitate the individuals under their care. The brother's obsession with what the world saw as his abnormal sexuality – his profound lack of self-acceptance – led him to retaliate with the full force of accusation and blame. It was evident the parents had read this book: he had published it under his own name, after all. The mother had been proud of the brother's achievements, the father says now, but it would not remotely have occurred to her to see herself in connection with them. It is the shock that is killing her. What kind of grown man walks around blaming his mother?

G does not tell the father that the brother regularly appears at debates and even on television, calumnising the parents and arguing for the sexual freedom of children. He is part of a coterie of intellectuals who hold the belief that the pleasure of the body is sovereign and should be liberated from all convention. It seems the childhood freedom they are arguing for is in fact the freedom for adults to have sexual congress with them. People are disgusted and shocked by this notion, but G's brother doesn't spend his time with such people. G does not involve himself in these arguments. For him, an adult is merely a corrupted child, who has availed himself of the weapons – and then the crutches – with which society is only too happy to supply him. It is all he sees, the child inside the adult's body, crippled and corrupted by money, fear, gluttony, conformity, addiction: he even sees the child inside his mother, lying on her deathbed. How, he wonders, did we become so evil? He sees that it is possible to live the span of a whole life and never once realise that the truth of oneself has been destroyed – not only possible but usual. In his films he delicately, obsessively tracks this relentless loss of innocence, a loss that occurs in moments of barely perceptible action and interaction. At the centre of his dramas there is very often a person who proves harder to corrupt, whose innocence is more shining and resilient than that of others. The sufferings and progressions of this person are his true subject. He has no doubt that his anonymity is what allows him to see what he sees. Because of it he has no investment in the game of life. He is a spy; his ego is exiled, at bay. Like the spy, the difficulty is that he can't make things happen – he just has to be sure he's there when they do.

This idea that G's brother has killed their mother has taken hold in the father so quickly that he is soon treating it as a matter of objective fact. The father himself takes no responsibility. The sight of the mother's withered, wordless body, her withdrawal from the field of action, is so unacceptable that someone must be to blame for it, and he has been trained to blame anyone and anything other than himself. Presently he asks about G's supposed teaching job and his life in the provincial town where he believes G still lives. He has never shown any interest in these subjects before: all his ambition was invested in G's brother. Now he is writhing, like someone who has backed the wrong horse in a race. It is with the greatest effort that G tolerates his father. Were it not for his mother, he isn't sure he would have taken the trouble to disguise his true identity. The thought occurs to him that perhaps he wouldn't have had to: perhaps she would have accepted him, protected him even, had she been left alone to care for him naturally. Instead her own oppression became his, the cruelty she had been offered became the cruelty she passed on. He detests men, detests all that they are. His belief is that women are the true creators: they are motivated to give, and in the generosity of their creativity they inadvertently make themselves slaves and henchmen. The creativity of men, which is not creativity at all but a mode of conquest, disgusts him.

The doctor comes. The mother is not going to recover. She will not be getting out of bed and resuming her activities. She has gone somewhere, to a kind of middle land between life and death, from which she cannot come back. There is no knowing how long she will spend there. G makes phone calls and rearranges his plans. He sits by the bed and waits while the light travels from one end of the room to the other.

Many of the objects around our mother's deathbed had existed for as long as we could remember. When we first entered her room we saw and recognised them more clearly than we recognised her. These objects contained our mother. They were more reliable and lasting than she was. It seemed impossible that she would die because she had never told the truth, but the objects told a different kind of truth. Their actual existence and their existence in memory were the same. She had imagined she was stronger than them, that she owned them, but in this element of consistency lay their victory over her. It was they that would commemorate her.

We were together again in our parents' house, as we had been in childhood, except that now our bodies were the used bodies of adults. We were frightened. We were frightened but we lacked the darting speed and lightness of children. We lacked the ability to conceal ourselves. We moved around uneasily with our garish voices and our creased, reddened faces and the passage of time seemed terrible and incomprehensible to us in the light of our fear. The prospect of our abandonment had never left us, and yet its realisation now had caught us somehow unawares. We gathered in doorways or corridors or the corners of rooms and dispersed again. We did not sit down. The door to the bedroom was frightening. We were still the children of the figure lying on the other side of it. Our fear of her and our fear of her death were difficult to distinguish from one another.

In the bedroom she lay in her nightdress as though on

a plinth. She appeared to be being sacrificed. Was it we who had demanded it? Was it our fault, our wish that she would die? Her face was a mask of bone offered to the ceiling. The thin matted hair lay around it on the pillow. We felt that we did not know her, that she was unknowable. We felt that we ought to save her. But we were children: we didn't have the power to save. Were we to worry about her? But who would worry about us, when she was gone? We remembered a day, when we were small, when she had been very unhappy. Our father had been at work. She had lain on her bed in her nightdress and cried and we had gathered around her trying to comfort her. We remembered the pure sorrow and pity we had felt. Now we were gathered again around her bed and what struck us was the loss of this purity. It had been squandered, or she had squandered it. We remembered what it was, to have felt so purely.

Our father's behaviour was disordered and occasionally violent: he was being turned upside down. He had the appearance of a malfunctioning machine. He stood at the foot of our mother's bed and shouted at her. He was angry with the nurses, who came and went in their cars. He talked about the food he wanted and wasn't getting. He wandered around the house at night, turning on the lights, turning the television on at full volume. It was evident that he continued to share the bed on which our mother lay. In the daytime he did not, as we did, stay at her bedside. Each time we came out of her room he asked us whether she was dead yet. He did not appear to want to save her. He was like an animal that had been flushed out of its cover: with her retreat he was steadily being exposed. Like her, he momentarily mistook death for freedom. He talked about the things he planned to do when she was gone, things she had prevented him from doing. But it was too late for him to do these things.

Her breathing was slow and noisy. Sometimes there were long interludes between the breaths and we wondered if she had died. Then she breathed again and the matter of death seemed consequently to have grown more complex and opaque. We did not know what death was. We did not know how to die. If not a natural cessation, what was it? What qualification or readiness was lacking here? The longer we sat and listened to her mechanical and aimless breaths, the more apparent the absence of nature became to us. Nature was not attending her deathbed, was not in this room nor anywhere near, had not been seen or asked after for many years. In fact we had no memory of nature at all and this, we began to suspect, was why we had no knowledge of death. There had been nothing natural in our dealings with our mother. We had been taught to suppress nature. We had been taught to regard the natural processes of our own bodies as disgusting. How were we expected to conjure death? Sometimes she would open her eyes and the glimmer of consciousness became visible. We had heard that in recognising death people recognised a greater mystery, the mystery of life. We had heard that these could be moments of revelation. But in her eyes there was no suggestion of revelation. What we saw in her eyes were the vestiges of her control of the story of her life. The difficulty lay in the extinguishing of the storyteller. How could she tell the story of her own death?

We thought that love might help her out of this difficulty. We thought love might show her how to die. Sitting by her bedside, we tried to offer love as we might have tried to communicate in a foreign language, clumsily but out of necessity. Ridiculous as we felt, we tried to be sincere. It struck us how naturally we spoke in our own language of love: in our love for our children, for instance, there was none of this clumsiness and constraint. Why did we love our children? How, when we had not inherited the language of love, had we learned to speak it? Perhaps, after all, we spoke it badly and ridiculously. It seemed all at once terrible to be us, terrible to be without origins in love, without language. Slowly we stopped trying to offer love to our mother. We stopped our awkward caresses and our unnatural words. We fell silent as the mechanical sound of her breathing came and went.

The nurses had said that she would shortly die but the days passed and she did not die. The problem, it seemed, was after all a problem not of nature nor of love but of truth. The truth was that they had stopped giving her nourishment. They had stopped giving her liquid. If it was unclear why her body should die by itself, this lack of sustenance gradually took on an inevitability of its own. She appeared to be dying of death, dying because it had been decided that she had to, dying because in the absence of love or nature there was no reason for her to remain alive. No one suggested that she should be given nourishment or liquid. No one suggested that she should endeavour to remain human and alert in the encounter with death. In fact death wasn't coming, and with the failure of death to arrive, a substitute seemed to be presenting itself: disposal.

We went away, back to our own lives. We left her with the agents of disposal, the nurses, our disordered father. We were told that one night, getting into bed, he had noticed that she had died and had got in beside her and gone to sleep. At the news of her death we felt nothing, and understood that to have felt nothing was the great-est tragedy that could have befallen us, for its effect on us could only be to reveal greater depths and breadths of non-feeling, such that it almost seemed to cancel us out. Since her whole life had been a fabrication, or a construction, we ourselves lacked a basis in reality. She had lied to us, even if only by not telling us the truth and by allowing us to be lied to through her: had we lied back, had we never let her see us or know us, we might have saved ourselves. Instead we had exposed ourselves and our needs to her. We had exposed our need for nature and love and truth, and our blind belief in her as their representative. We had hoped that one day she would be revealed to be their representative. Dimly we understood that she was no more than the product of the things that had happened to and formed her, but the operation of her self, her soul, remained for us a tantalising possibility. One day, we believed, she would step out of the artefact of her body and we would see her soul.

After the funeral we resumed our usual activities. When we happened to mention to people that our mother had died, their sympathy and concern were disturbing. It was on these occasions that we felt grief, or something that resembled grief. It was like the brutal turning of a rusty blade inside us. What we were grieving was the fact that nothing had changed or been resolved, and that there was no longer the chance to resolve it. We were full of a dark knowledge that had briefly surfaced and over which the waters of time were closing again.

We had obligations and responsibilities of our own. We travelled for work. In a northern city, in our free time, we went to a museum. It was late in the day, half an hour before closing, and we decided to see the temporary exhibition that was on display. We were surprised that we knew nothing about the artist but in fact there was nothing to know: he was virtually anonymous. For centuries his work had been mistaken for that of a far more famous artist of the same school, and once the misappropriation had been acknowledged his activities lay too far back in time to be reconstructed. There were only the paintings themselves in which to look for clues. The paintings were interiors and streetscapes. They possessed a great eeriness that was partly the result of their manufacture by an unknown hand and partly that of the strangeness of what they saw. They were often scenes in which apparently nothing was happening and where the basic formality of the captured moment was absent. In one, for instance, a middle-aged woman was sitting alone in an empty room reading a book. The room was full of a bare light but the windows behind her were dark: it was night-time. She was fleshy, well dressed, self-absorbed. This woman was alone in a way that was nearly impossible to represent – it might have been captured, for instance, on a security camera. Immersed in being herself, she was indifferent to how she was seen. This indifference was oddly familiar to us. How had someone observed her in that way, alone?

It was only after several moments that we noticed a face in one of the windows behind her. It was the face of a small child standing outside in the darkness. He was looking in at her but she didn't know he was there. She didn't care enough to know: he didn't matter to her. Yet he wanted something, was waiting out there in the dark for something. He wanted her to turn around and see him. In another painting of the same room, again at night, there was now a different woman sitting in the chair. She was leaning toward the dark window so that we could only see her back. On the other side of the window there was again the face of the little child alone in the darkness. The woman was waving at the child through the glass, her hand and face almost pressed to it, the chair nearly toppling with her enthusiasm. The child was smiling. We were told that this was the only example in this school of painting of a woman tipped forward in her chair to look through a window. But we had already recognised the rarity of love.

The next morning, in the hotel room, we stood at the window looking out at the curious devastation of dawn, its relentless casting of new light on old failures. We understood that the opportunity to disguise and transform ourselves had passed. We realised that the death of our mother's body meant that we now contained her, since she no longer had a container of her own. She was inside us, as once we had been inside her. The pane of glass between herself and us, between the dark of outside and the day of inside, had been broken. We recognised the ugliness of change; we embraced it, the litter-filled world where truth now lay. This grey reality, this meeting of darkness and light across shards of broken glass, was our beginning.

A NOTE ABOUT THE AUTHOR

Rachel Cusk is the author of *Second Place*, the Outline trilogy, the memoirs *A Life's Work* and *Aftermath*, and several other works of fiction and nonfiction. She is a Guggenheim Fellow. She lives in Paris.